Getting a grip on both her emotions and her traitorous body, Saana walked around the car on weak legs to the semicircular staircase leading to her front door.

"Well," she said, aware of Kenzie's gaze following her and refusing to meet it again. "This has been delightful, but I'm afraid it's time for you to leave."

She was two steps up when Kenzie replied. "Saana, I need your help."

Pausing, Saana felt the words echo between them. In fact, it was almost impossible to believe she'd heard them correctly.

Unable to resist, she looked over her shoulder, saying, "As surprising as it is to hear you, Miss Independent, say that, I'm sorry. I'm not interested in offering assistance."

Then, as she turned to climb to the next step, wanting to hurry now, to get away, she heard Kenzie say, "I'm pregnant with twins. And I really need your help."

And she froze where she stood, trying to process the words.

Dear Reader,

I suppose it should come as no surprise that I absolutely believe in love at first sight. That wonderful, soul-shaking moment when gazes meet, hearts collide and something in the universe shifts, falling beautifully into place.

Of course, I also know that the path to true love doesn't always run smoothly, but we writers need those ups and downs to give them the happily-ever-after we all crave.

Over the years, I've realized people who haven't met a romance writer sometimes think we have a rose-tinted worldview, but it's absolutely not true. Instead, most of us are pragmatists trying to make sense of a world that hasn't always seemed logical or been kind, and allow our readers a glimpse of what can be. We write happy families when our own have been dysfunctional, and about love when, sometimes, it's what we haven't found yet. I'm thankful for having my own love-at-first-sight moment thirty-plus years ago, and getting to relive it when I write a similar scene.

All of this to say, thank you for your support and kindness to me and all the authors whose books you read. I am hoping you'll love Saana and Kenzie's journey to their HEA as much as I enjoyed writing it!

Ann

TWIN BABIES
TO REUNITE THEM

ANN McINTOSH

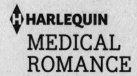

HARLEQUIN
MEDICAL
ROMANCE

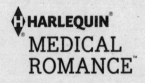

Recycling programs for this product may not exist in your area.

ISBN-13: 978-1-335-73794-6

Twin Babies to Reunite Them

Copyright © 2023 by Ann McIntosh

Harlequin Enterprises ULC
22 Adelaide St. West, 41st Floor
Toronto, Ontario M5H 4E3, Canada
www.Harlequin.com

Printed in U.S.A.

Ann McIntosh was born in the tropics, lived in the frozen north for a number of years and now resides in sunny central Florida with her husband. She's a proud mama to three grown children, and loves tea, crafting, animals (except reptiles!), bacon and the ocean. She believes in the power of romance to heal, inspire and provide hope in our complex world.

Books by Ann McIntosh

Harlequin Medical Romance

Carey Cove Midwives
Christmas Miracle on Their Doorstep

A Summer in São Paulo
Awakened by Her Brooding Brazilian

Surgeon Prince, Cinderella Bride
The Nurse's Christmas Temptation
Best Friend to Doctor Right
Christmas with Her Lost-and-Found Lover
Night Shifts with the Miami Doc
Island Fling with the Surgeon
Christmas Miracle in Jamaica
How to Heal the Surgeon's Heart
One-Night Fling in Positano

Visit the Author Profile page at Harlequin.com.

With thanks to Nicole and Heather, whose love, marriage and devotion to each other are an inspiration to everyone.

CHAPTER ONE

DR. SAANA AMIRI CHECKED her watch and suppressed a yawn. While the low-cost women's clinic only operated from Tuesday to Saturday, from four in the afternoon to nine at night, when coupled with her regular daytime practice, it made for long weeks. Thankfully, this would be the last patient of the night, and with the next day being Sunday, she could look forward to at least one day to recharge her batteries.

As she arrived at the examination-room door, she paused on hearing nurse Amanda Curry's voice from inside.

"Why on earth didn't you see a doctor long before this?"

It wasn't just the words, more so the hectoring tone that made Saana's hackles rise. The last thing the women coming to the clinic needed was to be berated by the very people they were depending on to help them. The hardships many of them suffered didn't need to be compounded by unsympathetic behavior on the part of the medical team.

With a quick rap on the door, she stepped into the room and took in the scene with a sweeping glance.

Nurse Curry stood with her hands on her hips, frowning at the patient, Mylie Nelson, who stared back with what could only be called a defensive glare on her pale, narrow face. Seated on the examination table, Mylie had one arm bent behind her back, hiding it from sight; nearby, in a kidney dish, was a small pile of soiled bandages. In the corner of the room lay a large, fully stuffed backpack, a small duffel bag—equally full—and a couple of shopping bags.

Before either of the other women could say anything else, Saana walked over to grab a pair of disposable gloves and interrupted the conversation.

"Hello, Ms. Nelson. I'm Dr. Amiri." Giving the nurse a cool glance, she continued, "Thank you, Nurse. I'll take over now."

Amanda Curry frowned, probably because of Saana's tone, but after a murmured agreement, she left the examination room. Apparently, though, she couldn't resist closing the door behind her with an ill-tempered snap.

Putting the nurse out of her mind, Saana turned to her patient and smiled.

"So, what can I do for you this evening?"

And there was no mistaking the reluctance with which the patient revealed the jagged wound on her arm.

As she examined the infected injury, Saana questioned how it had occurred, keeping her tone gentle and sympathetic as the story unfolded. Mylie had caught her arm on a piece of corrugated iron but, afraid to miss work, hadn't been able to have it tended to. Now, five days later, she hadn't been able to ignore it anymore.

Although she was sure there was more to the story, Saana took it at face value and was pleased when her patient relaxed.

The small mound of bags told the familiar tale of homelessness Saana had no trouble recognizing, but it was with women like Mylie in mind that she'd opened the clinic. Florida's mild winters attracted more than just snow birds, as the part-time, retired residents were called. Many transients who originally came south to avoid the northern cold ended up staying year-round.

"I'm going to need to clean the wound and tape it closed. I'll administer a tetanus shot, and you'll need to do a course of antibiotics," she told Mylie. "I can give you a voucher for the pharmacy, if you need one, and you have to take all the antibiotic tablets. Don't stop, even if your arm seems to be better. Are you allergic to penicillin or any other medications?"

By the time she'd finished with Mylie Nelson,

it was almost ten o'clock, and although the clinic officially closed at nine thirty, most of the staff were still on-site. Since it was standard operating procedure for everyone to leave at the same time, under the watchful eyes of the night security guard, Saana did a quick head count.

"We're one short," she said. "Who's missing?"

"Nurse Curry left already," one of the other nurses replied.

Saana tamped down her instinctive spurt of annoyance.

"Okay, let's get out of here," she said, hitching her tote bag a little higher onto her shoulder. "Thanks, everyone. Enjoy what's left of the weekend, and I'll see you all on Tuesday afternoon."

Once in her car, Saana sighed and pushed a strand of hair off her cheek. While she was tired, her muscles aching with fatigue, her brain was still running full steam.

Amanda Curry wasn't someone she wanted to work with. Over the three weeks the nurse had been at the clinic, Saana had noticed her condescending attitude toward both patients and other staff members, as though she felt them all beneath her. Saana had given the HR team very specific instructions about hiring staff, but although Nurse Curry didn't fit the bill, it wasn't their fault. One of the nurses originally hired two months ago when the clinic opened had become ill and took a leave of absence. Nurse Curry was a traveling nurse and had been sent by an agency to fill the temporary vacancy.

As Saana headed south on US 1, she decided to contact the agency to have Nurse Curry replaced. Using the onboard electronic system linked to her phone, she set herself a reminder for Monday morning. Not that she was likely to forget, but being methodical was an ingrained part of her personality.

A vehicle swerved into her lane, making her have to hit the brakes and suppress a curse. As usual on a Saturday night, the thoroughfare, which led into the downtown Melbourne area, was busy and the driving was sometimes erratic.

As the car in front of her slowed almost to a halt although there was nothing in front of it, Saana had the urge to pull out into the oncoming lane and overtake. After all, her sports car would easily zoom past the sedan, and the speed might alleviate some of the restless energy still firing through her system.

But even as her leg muscles tensed to hit the accelerator, she forced them to relax again.

Impulsiveness wasn't something she gave in to often now, especially after the spectacular mess she'd made the last time she indulged.

Saana shook her head abruptly, annoyed, and as if to prove the wisdom of not overtaking on the double yellow lines, she spotted a police car on the verge. She would have gotten a hefty ticket, for sure.

There. *Better safe than sorry* wasn't just a maxim but words to live by, so as to not get into trouble.

Of all kinds.

It was what her father had said when she'd told him her plan to open a low-cost clinic integrated with her already thriving medical practice.

"To be frank, I think it would be a mistake," he'd said. "What you're proposing would immediately become a drain on your resources, both professionally and—knowing you—personally too."

Twirling the stem of her wineglass between her fingers, she'd tried to figure out exactly what he was saying.

"The women of Brevard County need a place to go for testing and treatment when they don't have insurance," she'd replied, keeping her voice mild but strong, so he'd have no doubt she was serious about the project. "I have the means to help provide that for at least some of them."

"I'm not saying not to do it," Dad had replied, getting up to freshen his own drink. "But be cautious and realistic about what it will cost and how you can sustain such a project without damaging what you already have."

Saana had known what he was skirting around and bit back her instinctive urge to defend herself. Yes, in the past she'd sometimes jumped into things without thinking them through, but it had been a while since she'd learned not to be so rash.

Two years, ten months and twenty-six days, to be precise. But who was counting?

Clearly, she was.

Of course, she'd taken his advice and consulted lawyers, accountants and other practitioners, especially those who specialized in low-cost care. In the end, she'd taken some of the inheritance from her grandfather and set up a trust. Then she'd hired a firm to both manage the trust and prioritize fundraising so she wouldn't need to deal with either.

All she was interested in was practicing medicine.

The first major fundraiser was scheduled in a month's time, at her parent's house, and Saana was frankly dreading it.

On being told about the fundraising party, Mom had insisted it take place at the Amiris' Merritt Island estate, where Saana had grown up. Between Mom and the party coordinator, it sounded like a magical scene had been planned, and the guest list of wealthy socialites would hopefully be moved to donate.

Saana couldn't help twisting her lips at the irony.

Thousands of dollars spent on champagne,

canapés and a gourmet meal to entice people to give money to a cause that could have benefited greatly from that initial outlay. Oh, she understood it; after all, she'd grown up in this rarefied existence, where tax write-offs and social visibility trumped genuine generosity. But it still didn't sit well.

Yet she knew she had to play the game if the clinic was to be a success and outlive her, the way she hoped it would.

It was never too early to think about the legacy you'd leave behind.

She turned off US 1 and, after going over the Melbourne Causeway into Indialantic, drove slowly through the far quieter streets of her neighborhood. Smaller cottages began to give way to larger lots and houses the nearer she got to her home on the Indian River Lagoon. As soon as she was close enough, Saana hit the button to open the security gate, getting to it just as the tall wrought iron wings opened just enough for her car to go through. She was halfway down her curved driveway when she noticed a dark-colored sedan parked, facing out, at the front right-hand side of the house.

Instinctively, she eased off the gas, slowing the vehicle down as she put her finger on the panic button located on the steering wheel.

She wasn't expecting anyone, and no one had

rung at the gate to be let in, because the request would have popped up on her phone.

Who was this, and how had they gained entrance to her property?

Then, before she could call for help, the driver's-side door of the other car opened, and someone stepped out.

Saana hit the brakes, and her hand dropped down into her lap, boneless.

Kenzie?

The other woman stood, unmoving, behind the car door, watching Saana's vehicle, too far away for her expression to be visible. Saana was glad for the distance.

Between one breath and the next, all the carefully constructed barriers she'd built around her heart crumbled, and she was falling apart. Battered by a rush of complex and nauseating emotions she couldn't name and didn't want Kenzie to see.

Time slowed as Saana began to shake and her brain went into hyperdrive, trying to figure out what to do.

She could hit the gate button again and reverse away through it.

Drive around to the garage and let herself into the house, ignoring and leaving Kenzie where she was.

Or I can brazen it out. Show her I don't care

why she's here—only that she needs to leave again.

That thought somehow steadied her, easing the band of ice constricting her chest, allowing her to breathe as a rush of heated anger overrode everything else.

How dare she just appear like this, as though no time has passed and nothing has happened?

As if she hadn't broken Saana's heart and destroyed her faith in herself and love?

Now Saana could ascribe the trembling of her hands and wild cadence of her heart to rage, and it firmed her determination not to let Kenzie's appearance get the better of her.

After taking a couple of deep breaths, she eased off the brake and drove forward, parking her car parallel to Kenzie's. Getting out, she looked over the roof of both vehicles at her estranged wife.

"McKenzie." Saana wasn't sure how she kept her voice so cool and steady but was proud of the effect. "How did you get in here?"

Safer than asking why she was there.

Kenzie shook her head slightly, her lush lips kicking up a hint at the corners.

"If you'd changed the security code, I'd still be outside."

She'd meant to change the code. Just like she'd meant to file for divorce once she'd gotten it into her thick skull that Kenzie Bonham wasn't coming back.

Neither of those chores had been crossed off her to-do list.

Refusing to even contemplate why that was, and trying not to let the sound of that sweet drawl insinuate itself into her psyche, she shrugged lightly. Closing her car door, she clutched her tote bag so tightly the leather straps dug into her palm.

"If I'd had even an inkling that you'd turn up like this, I would have."

Was that a flash of pain that shot across Kenzie's face at her cold pronouncement? If so, Saana felt not a shred of remorse. She hoped the barb *had* struck home since Kenzie absolutely deserved whatever discomfort she felt.

Silence fell between them for a moment, and Saana found her gaze fixed on Kenzie's face. Unable to tear it away, she took in what she could see of the other woman, the thundering of her heart giving the moment far too much weight.

Kenzie's face looked narrower, the satiny, cocoa-hued skin stretched a little tighter than usual, her cheeks not as full as Saana remembered. Her hair was longer, worn in a mass of corkscrew curls that moved gently in the breeze blowing from the ocean, held back by a simple black bandeau. Kenzie had beautiful eyes. Dark brown, gleaming with intelligence and often with ready laughter. Although she was too far away to see the expression in them, Saana's memory supplied the details—the way looking into them was like drowning in love and desire.

And those lips…

A tidal wave of arousal crashed over Saana as her gaze dropped to that full, wide mouth—unsmiling now, but no less sinfully sexy for that fact.

Against her will, her head suddenly filled with scenes, scents, sensations of being held in Kenzie's arms. There, her every sensual need had been met, ecstasy lifting her higher and higher, until it became irresistible and she was flung into the stratosphere.

Taken to the stars.

Suddenly weak-kneed once more, Saana knew it was time to bring this surreal encounter to an end. The sustaining anger had waned, leaving her floundering and sad.

But she wouldn't allow that to show.

The one person she'd ever completely trusted had betrayed her and deserved nothing but cool dismissal.

Getting a grip on both her emotions and her traitorous body, and although her legs still felt weak, she walked around the car to the semicircular staircase leading to her front door.

"Well," she said, aware of Kenzie's gaze following her and refusing to meet it again. "This has been delightful, but I'm afraid it's time for you to leave."

She was two steps up when Kenzie replied.

"Saana, I need your help."

Pausing, Saana felt the words echo, shockingly, between them. In fact, it was almost impossible to believe she'd heard them correctly.

Unable to resist, she looked over her shoulder, saying, "As surprising as it is to hear you, Miss Independence, say that, I'm sorry. I'm not interested in offering assistance."

Then, as she turned to climb to the next step—wanting to hurry now, to get away—she heard Kenzie say, "I'm pregnant with twins. And I really need your help."

She froze where she stood, trying to process the words, her first impulse to spin around and look at Kenzie to judge whether she was telling the truth or not. To let loose all the questions firing around her brain.

Pregnant? By whom? Had she started a new relationship without telling Saana? Decided she wanted a family with someone other than the wife she'd promised to love and cherish always but had then left behind?

The hand she'd laid on the banister tightened until even the bones hurt. Behind her, a car door slammed, and her already racing heart sped up even more. If she spun around now, Kenzie would be completely visible, and perhaps Saana could figure out how far along she was.

But hadn't she learned her lesson? Impulsive behavior—which she knew herself to be prone to on occasion—not only often got her in trouble but had, more specifically, gotten her into the present situation.

They were standing, watching the water show outside the Bellagio, Kenzie's arm around Saana's shoulders, their heads close together. It came to Saana that she'd never been happier. Never felt more secure, comfortable—loved. She'd only known Kenzie for five days, and these were the last few hours they'd spend together before the other woman went back to Texas.

"Marry me," she said, unable to stop the words from emerging, though she knew it was crazy to even suggest it. "I can't imagine my life without you now."

Those dark, gleaming eyes, wide with surprise, turned to search her gaze, and Saana's heart beat so hard she felt sick.

Then, shockingly, she said, "Yes..."

But it had all turned out to be a mistake. A mirage.

One she didn't dare allow herself to be pulled back into, lest she find it impossible to extricate herself.

"No..."

But it came out like a sigh, too quiet to be

heard by the woman standing behind her, and even as she said it, Saana knew she'd have to force herself to mean it.

That the emotion Kenzie had awoken in her had never faded but now would have to be ruthlessly suppressed.

CHAPTER TWO

KENZIE LEANED AGAINST the side of her car, needing the support to stay on her feet.

You'd think she'd be steadier. After all, she'd had lots of time to prepare for these moments, from the first stomach-churning instant she realized the trouble she was in to the two-day journey from San Antonio to Indialantic. It was a desperate plan to begin with, and she knew it may not work, but she'd been determined to at least try.

And she'd reminded herself, over and over, that her feelings for Saana didn't matter. Not anymore. Not when she was responsible for the lives growing in her belly.

The babies had to come first. Always.

Yet thinking she was ready to face whatever she found here in Florida had been a lie.

Just the approach of Saana's vehicle created a wave of such mingled love, desire and sadness that it had taken all her strength to get out of the car. Then, on seeing her wife again, it had taken every ounce of control to keep her voice even, when all she wanted to do was round the vehicles and pull Saana into her arms.

Kiss her, never wanting to stop.

Find home again in her embrace.

Now, looking up at Saana where she stood on the staircase, Kenzie was once more reminded of all the reasons why their marriage didn't—couldn't—work.

Saana was so elegant, so incredibly beautiful that Kenzie could hardly believe she'd ever been lucky enough to touch her, much less be married to her.

Even casually dressed in a slim-fitting pair of tailored trousers and a long-sleeve cotton shirt, simple gold hoops in her ears, she was all graceful sophistication. Saana had cut her hair since the last time Kenzie saw her, and thick, dark strands feathered around her face, emphasizing the gorgeous bone structure and wide-set hazel eyes. The honey-toned skin, as smooth as velvet, just begged to be touched.

In contrast, Kenzie's low-slung jeans, sleeveless and shapeless plaid shirt and dusty cowboy boots proclaimed, loud and clear, her country-girl heritage.

And it wasn't hard to feel, once again, that she didn't belong here in this hoity-toity neighborhood, where people weren't just rich but insanely wealthy.

That was a concept Kenzie had never considered until moving to Florida to be with Saana over two and a half years ago. Up until then, in her mind, people were either rich, middle-class or poor. Sure, she knew there were gazillionaires, but to her they were sort of like unicorns—mythical and never to be experienced in real life.

Once she'd gotten a taste of what wealth truly meant, she knew she didn't understand it. Nor would she ever truly fit in, and there was no way to explain that to Saana fully without hurting her. Kenzie had been careful not to tell her wife about the rudeness and snubs she'd experienced from Saana's friends.

It had taken her months after leaving to realize just how beaten down she'd been by those interactions; how low her self-esteem had fallen. Not to mention how Kenzie being with her would be detrimental to Saana's image.

If she couldn't be an asset to her wife, then it was better she stay out of Saana's life.

No. If there was any other way to protect the babies, she wouldn't be here.

No matter how much she loved Saana—wanted, *needed* her—it would never be enough. She couldn't live her life constantly feeling inferior to her surroundings. A fish out of water. A source of embarrassment to the woman she loved.

A woman who hadn't moved in over a minute.

"Saana—"

Saana's hand chopped downwards, obviously to cut off whatever Kenzie was going to say, and when she turned around, Kenzie felt a trickle, like melting snow, down her spine.

Her face was calm, untroubled, but her eyes—flashing with anger—belied that unconcerned facade.

"Your condition has nothing to do with me," she said, her voice as cold as the sensation growing in Kenzie's chest. "I think you should leave."

The curt dismissal fired through the air like bullets but was nothing less than Kenzie knew she deserved. Although she wanted to walk—no, *run*—away, that wasn't an option.

"Please, Saana. Will you at least let me explain what's going on?" God, why was it so hard to ask for help, especially from the regal woman in front of her? Didn't Saana know how difficult this was? How behind the eight ball Kenzie had to be to even ask? "You know I wouldn't be here if I had any alternative."

Saana's eyes narrowed, and her lips tightened, and for an instant Kenzie thought she might, for once, lose control. Maybe even shout or curse. Show some outward evidence of strong emotion rather than keep it all inside.

Then her expression smoothed out, and she gave one of her characteristic shrugs, shoulders moving forward, then back, her chin tilting to one side.

"I'll hear you out, but your problems aren't my concern, so don't expect my help."

Then she turned and walked slowly up the stairs, like a queen having dismissed her subject, and Kenzie trailed behind, scared but determined.

Only the babies mattered, she reminded herself, even as her heart ached with sadness and with love for the woman walking in front of her.

The house loomed before her, as unwelcoming as she remembered. It was a mansion, with so many rooms some of them were closed up because they were unused. Filled with things that were beautiful and obviously expensive, it had felt like a showpiece rather than a home to Kenzie. She'd been afraid to touch anything, hadn't wanted to put up her feet anywhere.

The only place that held any meaning to her here was upstairs, in the bedroom. There, Saana and she had explored each other with the type of abandon Kenzie hadn't expected but had relished.

She shivered, trying to push thoughts of their lovemaking aside, and now the interior of the house seemed to scowl at her as she stepped inside and closed the door. Her stomach clenched, and her hands started trembling. Stuffing her fingers into her pockets, she called out to Saana, who had continued on into the sitting room.

"I just have to run to the john."

"You know where it is," came the cool reply.

Yeah, she did. She'd lived in the house for ten months, and nothing seemed to have changed in the two years since she'd left.

With her overwrought nerves, the clack of her boots across the marble foyer sounded extraordinarily loud, each echoing pop seeming to emphasize her unsuitability to be in the house. It was a momentary relief to step onto the thick runner that covered the floor of the hall, and then Kenzie couldn't help glancing back to see if she was leaving dirty footprints on the cream fabric.

"Get over yourself," she muttered under her breath as she opened the door into the powder room and flicked on the light, illuminating a space larger than most people's bedrooms. If she was to have any hope of convincing Saana to help her, she'd need to move past her little ego trip and be logical.

Now wasn't the time to allow the nagging sense of unworthiness that had dogged her life here to take over.

Saana had closed herself away, all emotion locked tight, and it would take everything Kenzie had to break through that barrier to gain her sympathy. And without doing that, there was no way Saana would agree to help.

The unreality of the situation suddenly struck her anew as she tugged down her jeans and sat on the john, then leaned forward to put her hands on either side of her head.

Who could have known a random encounter in Las Vegas would have led to this moment?

Their relationship had, at the beginning, seemed like an extension of the fantastical aura surrounding her all-expenses-paid seven-night trip. Kenzie had never won anything in her life and had entered the radio-station contest on a whim. Flying into Vegas, seeing the lights beneath the wing, had made her not even care that she'd been guilted into taking Ashley with her instead of the friend she'd originally wanted to. Nor had her cousin's words, as they stood outside the hotel, felt like more than a pinprick.

"Stop gaping, Kenz. You look like even more of a hick than you are right now. Take my bag up to the room, will you? I'm heading to the casino."

She was used to Ashley's nonsense and hadn't wanted the hassle of an argument, so she'd done as commanded and spent most of that evening walking the strip, just taking in the sights.

Then, the next morning, she'd met Saana.

It had seemed totally right.

Despite the obvious differences between them—Kenzie had known right away that Saana was way too good for her—they'd also had a lot in common. They were both in medicine and loved romantic comedies, real Mexican food, strawberry everything and watching ice-skating. Even their differences had seemed more amusing than barriers to their holiday romance. They'd argued over the best types of music and books, which led to them sharing headphones, faces close together so they breathed each other in.

Everyone else on the tour bus could have disappeared right then and there, and neither of them would have noticed. Or cared.

Back then, Saana had seemed so open and free. The only hint of reticence had arisen when Kenzie—who, by then, wanted the other woman more than her next breath—had initiated their first kiss. For a brief instant, Saana had stiffened, her lips unmoving against Kenzie's. Thinking she wasn't into it, Kenzie had started to pull away—but just then Saana had pulled her closer, and that delicious mouth opened, accepting the entrance of Kenzie's tongue.

Later on, she realized what she'd seen as shyness about sex was really just Saana expressing a preference for submission. While to the outside world she presented a confident, no-nonsense facade, in bed she preferred to surrender and be told what to do. It had been so in-line with Kenzie's own more dominant style that she'd seen it as a perfect match.

Lying in bed, limbs twisted around each other, Kenzie had initiated a conversation on the topic, wanting to know everything she could about the fascinating woman she was falling for.

"I was a bit of a late bloomer," Saana had admitted. "I spent all my time trying to be the perfect daughter and granddaughter, the very best student, and sometimes I think it was because I was confused about my sexuality. I knew the guys I was dating weren't really fulfilling me, but because I'd spent so much time with my grandparents, I had a very conventional attitude toward sex."

Stroking her hair, Kenzie had asked, "When did you figure it all out?"

"In my mid-twenties, after being away from home for a while. I thought maybe I was bi, because I don't dislike being with men, but then I had an affair with a female classmate, and that was it."

Kenzie had tamped down the little rush of jealousy that twisted in her belly and the thought that she wished she'd been Saana's first. "Was it hard, coming out to your family?"

Saana had shifted, rolling over and propping herself up on her elbow so she was looking into Kenzie's eyes. "Not really. They're good people, with open minds and hearts. The hardest part for me was figuring the rest of it out. Especially when I got told that I was boring in bed."

Kenzie had been unable to prevent the little

bark of laughter breaking from her throat at the thought.

"You know better now, don't you?" Kenzie had said, sliding down in the bed so she was flat on her back and cupping a hand around the back of Saana's neck. "Or will I have to prove to you that you're anything but boring?"

Saana's eyelids had drooped, veiling her gaze, but she couldn't hide the flush staining her cheeks when Kenzie licked her lips…

"Stop, stop, stop," Kenzie told herself, getting up and straightening her clothes with hands that had once more grown shaky at the memory of how that night had gone. "This isn't helping."

Maybe it would be better to remember arriving at this unwelcoming mausoleum and finding out that Saana was even more above her pay grade than Kenzie could ever have imagined.

It was as if she could hear Aunt Lena's voice in her head again, as she had back then.

"Honey, I don't know what kind of hoodoo this woman cast over you, but getting married and leaving everyone you know behind after only knowing someone for six days is madness. Are you sure it's not some kinda scam?"

Kenzie hadn't known whether to laugh or get angry. "I looked her up on the internet, Auntie. She's legit a doctor in Florida, just about to open up her own clinic. I can't see why *she'd* want to scam *me*."

Aunt Lena had shaken her head, the sadness on her face heartbreaking. "Well, I hope I'm wrong, but I think you're makin' a big mistake. Just remember that if things don't work out, you can always come back here."

In hindsight, she should have taken those prophetic words to heart and kept her big butt in Texas. Not that doing so would have changed anything, really.

She would still be heartbroken by the loss of Saana and probably still pregnant.

The babies. You gotta forget everything else and concentrate on them.

Staring at her reflection in the mirror, she repeated the words one more time in her head and then added softly, out loud, "Remember, you're not plannin' to be here forever. Just long enough to straighten everything out. I love her, but we don't belong here. Remember that, okay?"

And she'd have to remind herself continuously just how impossible it had been to fit into Saana's life back then and how depressed and dispirited she'd been when she finally left. For the sake of her unborn children, she couldn't allow herself to get back to that state.

This time, if she ended up staying, it would be different.

It *had* to be.

CHAPTER THREE

I SHOULDN'T HAVE let her come in.

Saana stood by one of the living room windows, looking past her own reflection to the gardens, lit for the night by low spotlights, mentally kicking herself for agreeing to hear Kenzie out.

It was outrageous for her to show back up like this, asking for some type of favor, ripping the dressing off the wounds she'd inflicted.

Making Saana remember all the things she'd tried so hard to forget.

How it felt to be happy. In love. Content in a way she'd never been before.

All I need to remember is the pain.

That would bolster her against whatever pleas Kenzie might make.

There was the sound of the powder room door opening down the hallway, the tap of Kenzie's boots on the hardwood floor as she came into the formal living room, but Saana didn't turn around.

"I needed that, badly," Kenzie said, and the

sound of her voice made goose bumps fire out over Saana's back, chest and down her arms. A heated rush of arousal tightened her nipples and had tingling desire flooding her belly.

Get a hold of yourself.

Putting a bored expression on her face, she finally looked over at the younger woman, raising her eyebrows.

"Did you drive straight through?"

"I didn't think it would be wise." Kenzie hadn't sat down. In fact, she was hovering just inside the doorway, poised as though unsure whether to come in or not. "I stopped overnight in Pensacola."

Such banal conversation, ignoring the fact the air between them was thick with tension. Muffling a sigh, Saana walked over to an armchair. As she sat, she gestured to the nearby couch.

"Sit down, and let's get this over with."

She'd been trying not to look too closely at Kenzie but couldn't seem to stop her gaze from roaming over the curves and valleys of the other woman's body. Looking for the differences, she told herself. Trying to gauge how far along she was in her pregnancy.

But that really wasn't what registered.

Instead, she noted the sweet swing of Kenzie's hips as she strode across the room, the innate grace of her movements and the way she ran her hands down the outer seams of her jeans. She always complained about how sweaty her palms could get, making it a sure sign of nerves.

And the renewed burst of heat in Saana's belly had nothing to do with anger. Instead, it stemmed from the intimate memories she'd refused to let herself dwell on but now battered at her control.

The ones that arose in her dreams and left her twisting with unslaked desire.

Pushing them aside, she frowned across at Kenzie.

"Well?"

Kenzie rubbed a hand across her mouth, and Saana could see weariness in the movement. In the past, Kenzie had always been easy to read, her thoughts writ plain on her face and in her eyes. She'd been easygoing by nature, slow to anger, hard to rile, so there was seldom any reason for her to hide her emotions. Now Saana realized there was a barrier between them, making her strain to parse out what, exactly, the other woman was feeling.

"A year ago, my cousin Ashley asked me to be her surrogate."

Saana held up her hand, stopping the recitation. "This is the cousin who had cancer as a young woman?"

Kenzie nodded. "Yeah, that cousin. The treatment made her infertile, and she wanted me to donate eggs as well."

Saana didn't comment, but she remembered

Kenzie saying Ashley was spoiled rotten and always wanted her own way over everything.

"I initially told her I wasn't interested, but then…" Kenzie looked down for a moment, her fingers curling into her palms on her lap. "Well, let's just say I finally agreed to do it."

"Why?"

Kenzie looked up, her brows pinched in, wrinkling the skin above her nose.

"Does it matter?"

Saana smoothed one hand down the opposite sleeve thoughtfully. Kenzie's resistance to being questioned made Saana want to push at the other woman in a way she knew she'd hate.

Shrugging, she replied, "If you don't want to tell me, then I guess the conversation is over."

Kenzie's lips tightened in annoyance, but then she inhaled deeply, clearing trying to take control of her temper. That in itself showed how emotional she was, since anger was usually her last defense. When she'd exhaled, she met and held Saana's gaze.

"Aunt Lena was dying, and she asked me to do it. She said Ashley's husband, Darryl, was a good man and would take care of his family." She blinked rapidly, clearing the moisture that had gathered in her eyes. "I knew that was true, so even though I also knew Ashley probably wouldn't be a very good mother, I agreed to the IVF, using Darryl's sperm."

There was no need to question that decision. Kenzie's aunt had raised her from when she was very young, and it had been obvious how much Kenzie loved her. If Lena had asked it, and it was at all possible, Kenzie would do it.

A situation her cousin Ashley probably hadn't hesitated to exploit. From what Kenzie had said in the past, Lena had done everything she could to make Ashley's life comfortable, probably out of a misplaced sense of guilt over her daughter's illness. And Ashley had taken every advantage of the situation.

In fact, when Kenzie and Saana had met in Las Vegas, Ashley had been there, too, because Lena had asked Kenzie to take her cousin on the trip. If she hadn't, she and Kenzie probably would never have gotten together, since Ashley spent all her time in the casino, leaving Kenzie to her own devices.

If Kenzie had been with the friend she'd initially wanted to take, she wouldn't have been alone on the bus tour. Would most likely have been unavailable to Saana.

Memories of that week tried to impose themselves on her, but Saana shook them off fiercely.

This was no time to contemplate the joys of the past, and even though the sound of Lena's name sent a jagged pain through Saana's chest, she found herself saying, "I'm sorry for your loss." Then, not wanting sentimentality to come too strongly into the conversation, she asked, "So what happened?"

"I got pregnant during the first cycle of IVF, with the twins. But when I was twenty weeks along, Darryl, whose family owns a technical-supply company for the oil industry, was killed in a freak accident on the oil platform he was visiting."

She paused, rubbing her hand over her mouth again, and Saana felt a pang of sympathy.

"That must have been a shock."

Kenzie nodded and closed her eyes for a moment, as though reliving the moment.

"It was, but there was worse to come. Right after the funeral, Ashley told me she didn't want the babies. She'd never really wanted to be a mother; had only agreed to the arrangement to make Darryl happy."

Kenzie bit her lower lip, her gaze affixed to Saana's, probably waiting for a reaction or question, but although there were many things Saana wanted to ask, she kept silent.

It wasn't her job to make any of this easier.

After a moment, Kenzie continued. "Of course, I decided to keep them, and Ashley signed away her rights."

Then she looked down at her lap, and Saana knew they were getting to the crux of the discussion. Yet there was a part of her that didn't want to hear the rest—that was whispering warnings about the pain she was opening herself up to just by engaging.

Rising abruptly, she walked over to the sideboard to pick up the decanter of brandy. As she poured a splash into a snifter, she was about to offer Kenzie some when she remembered her condition, and the reality of it slammed home.

They'd never gotten around to discussing children during their brief, impetuous marriage, but in the back of her mind, Saana had imagined them going through the process. Deciding which of them would carry the baby, picking a donor, helping each other through the IVF, lovingly growing their family.

Together.

Another dream shattered.

Her hand was trembling when she set down the decanter and, without turning around, she asked, "Can I offer you some water or juice?"

Waiting for Kenzie's reply was a good way to give herself a moment or two more to get her emotions under control.

"No." The reply was abrupt, and Kenzie's voice sounded high and strained, as though she, too, had had enough of the stressful encounter. "Saana, listen—Darryl's parents have filed suit to gain custody of my babies when they're born."

She considered that for a moment, trying to work out the ramifications, to figure out just where she, of all people, came into it.

"So what do you want from me?" There could really only be one answer. "Money?"

The sound Kenzie made was impossible to interpret, especially with Saana's back still turned, but sounded like an outraged bark of laughter. Almost manic in nature.

"Hell no. Darryl gave me a lump sum of money when I agreed to the IVF, and even if he hadn't, I make—well, up until two weeks ago *made*—enough to support myself and my children."

She should have known better. The one thing Kenzie had never seemed interested in was Saana's considerable fortune. In fact, it seemed to have been something of an unpleasant surprise when Kenzie had found out exactly how wealthy her new wife was.

Taking a sip of her brandy, hoping the liquor's burn would steady her nerves, Saana finally turned to face Kenzie again. Leaning back against the sideboard, she braced herself, while the thunder of her heart in her ears made her voice sound far away.

"So what *do* you want?"

Kenzie stood up, seemingly no longer able to stay still, but instead of coming nearer to Saana, she walked away, toward the door.

Was she leaving?

It should have been a relief, but Saana had to stop herself from calling her back.

Then Kenzie turned on her heel to face Saana again and ran both hands down the outer seams of her jeans. Even from across the room, Saana could see the deep inhalation the other woman took, and then, in the midst of a long, rushing exhalation, she said, "I need you to pretend for the court that our marriage is solid and we'll be providing a good home environment for the babies."

And for the second time that evening, Saana's heart stuttered, a cold void opening in her belly as she stared in disbelief at the love of her life and her greatest heartbreak.

It took everything she had to hold on to her cool and not rage at Kenzie for even thinking up such a crazy, dangerous plan. Not to mention the sheer gall it took, after walking out on their marriage, to waltz back in and suggest they could pretend all was well between them. Just the thought of having Kenzie back in the house—back in her life—sent Saana's brain into a spin and her body into hyperdrive.

Yet, somehow, she stayed impassive and simply said, "No."

Kenzie had seen this side of Saana before. The coldly ruthless side she usually employed only when politeness, reason and all other lesser forms of discussion had failed.

Yet she'd never been the target of it, and that

one icy word stung more than anything else she'd experienced that night.

But she couldn't allow Saana's attitude to deter her, even if the entire venture seemed like a lost cause. This was too important to take her refusal without a fight.

"Saana…"

The other woman turned away, putting the glass to her lips and tipping the entire finger of booze into her mouth. That uncharacteristic move gave Kenzie a tiny glimmer of hope.

Saana hardly drank anything more than a glass or two of wine.

"Darryl's parents are rich and well-connected in San Antonio. They've already laid out their argument, and my lawyer says it might very well work." The words tripped over each other as Kenzie tried to make her own case. "They said I was only ever meant to be a surrogate and had agreed to hand over the babies to Darryl and Ashley, so I shouldn't try to argue that now I want these children for myself."

Saana didn't seem to even be listening. Instead, she'd picked back up the decanter and was pouring herself another finger of whatever it was she was drinking.

"I'm just a poor nurse," Kenzie continued, making no effort to disguise her fear. Her desperation. "I don't own a house or have a lot of resources. Mr. and Mrs. Beauchamp know that."

"You should ask your cousin for her help." Saana could have been discussing the weather, her tone flat and disinterested. "I'm assuming she inherited her husband's estate and isn't hurting for resources. Since she was the one who put you in this position, the least she could do is help to get you out of it."

The familiar anger she felt whenever she thought about Ashley's complete lack of interest colored her voice when Kenzie replied.

"She doesn't give a damn. As far as she's concerned, she doesn't see the problem. Her advice was simply to hand the babies over after they're born and walk away."

Swirling the alcohol in her glass around and around, Saana shrugged lightly.

"Maybe that's the best thing for you to do. After all, from what you've said, the Beauchamps raised their son well, and they can give the children whatever they need to thrive."

Balling her hands into fists until her short nails dug into her palms, Kenzie fought for control.

"That's not an option," she said, hearing her voice waver and despising herself for it. "Once Darryl died, I knew I had to take responsibility for the twins. After all, they're mine too."

Something flashed behind Saana's eyes, and her lips tightened, but all she did was shrug again.

"Then there's the argument you need to make

when you go to court. It will probably be cut-and-dried. You donated the eggs, ergo the children are as much yours as Darryl's. If he's not here to take care of them, the responsibility is yours, and you're willing to take it on. I doubt the court would deny you that right."

Unable to stand still, Kenzie paced across the room, her heart hammering, fear stalking right along beside her. When she got to the French doors leading out onto the terrace, she paused, staring out into the darkness. In the distance, the lagoon gleamed as moonlight touched the waves, while the lights from buildings on the landward side sent slivers of silver onto the water.

All this she noticed vaguely while she scrambled for a stronger argument to convince Saana.

What more could she say—what could she do—to get the help she knew, in her heart and soul, was necessary?

The Beauchamps were determined to get their grandchildren and, in a way, she couldn't blame them. They'd lost their son, and the twins were the last connection they had to him. If she were in their position, Kenzie wondered if she wouldn't do the same thing too. Fight for the right to take and raise the babies since Darryl had lost the chance to do it himself.

And they had the resources and the connections to sway the court to their side, while Kenzie...

Well, all she had was the bone-deep knowledge that these children were hers and she'd move heaven and hell to keep them and raise them.

She already loved them.

From the first flutters of life, which, coincidentally, came just a few days after Darryl's death, something warm and sweet had bloomed in her chest, and she'd known. It had made her cry, that precious moment. She—who never cried, who'd trained herself to be strong in every circumstance—had sobbed like a child, and she'd made a promise to herself, the twins and to Darryl that she'd be there for them.

That she'd be a good mother and give them the maternal love she'd never had.

Bolstered by that thought, she turned just in time to see Saana down the last of her drink and put the glass down on the sideboard with a little snap.

"McKenzie, I meant what I said: I cannot help you."

"Can't? Or won't?" she fired back, her stomach twisting with disappointment and that never-ending fear.

Again, that dismissive shrug, which made Kenzie want to scream.

"Is there a distinction I'm missing?" Before Kenzie could reply, Saana chopped her hand through the air. "It doesn't really matter. You got yourself into this position, and you'll have to work it out yourself."

She headed for the door, then paused momentarily to add, "If you need a place to stay tonight—by all means, use the pool house, but I expect you to leave in the morning."

Then she strode out of the room, and Kenzie stayed where she was. It was only until she heard Saana's bedroom door close on the floor above that she moved, sinking down onto the floor and resting her cheek against the glass door.

Shaking.

Once more fighting tears.

What do I do now?

CHAPTER FOUR

HAD A NIGHT ever seemed so long? Saana couldn't think of another that had stretched on—pain-filled and debilitating—as though never to end, except for the night after Kenzie had walked away from their marriage.

Yet this one had been different, Saana realized as she sat on the edge of her bed and contemplated the hours just passed. Two years ago, she'd curled into a ball, arms wrapped around her belly, trying to hold herself in one piece. Although part of her had held on to the hope Kenzie would come back, she'd cried until, devoid of even one more tear, exhaustion had dragged her into sleep. In comparison, last night she'd been too wired and angry to doze for more than a few minutes at a time, her brain spinning like a top with what she should do.

Go downstairs and tell Kenzie to leave immediately.

Follow her to the pool house and demand to know the real reason she'd decided to end the marriage. It wasn't the first time Saana had been cruelly rejected by a lover, but she'd been so head over heels for Kenzie that her leaving had shattered whatever confidence Saana had. Didn't she deserve to know what it was about her that made her unlovable?

And then there was the venal part of her brain, which didn't seem concerned with *why*s and *wherefore*s but kept sending erotic messages to the rest of her body. All it was interested in was the potential ecstasy Kenzie could so effortlessly provide if Saana were willing to demand it… Maybe in exchange for the help the other woman had asked for?

That idea was so ridiculous Saana had scoffed at herself.

From the moment Kenzie's lips had touched hers in Vegas, Saana had been lost. And when she'd realized Kenzie instinctively understood exactly how to take Saana past pleasure to the heights of ecstasy, there had been no looking back. No other lover had ever figured out the perfect mix of control and complicity that rendered Saana compliant and undone by need.

Wrestling with the combination of anger and desire had made the night seem to stretch to eternity, and she'd paced back and forth, emotions like a tornado tearing through her mind and body.

Now, as she made her way into the bathroom

to clean her teeth, she was no closer to any kind of reconciliation with her feelings, which seemed volatile enough to cause an explosion.

She'd never considered herself an emotional person. To her, life was something to enjoy, work hard at, think seriously about, but she'd never felt *immersed* in it the way she'd observed others to be. Yes, there were highs and lows, but she'd never wailed over a lost relationship, gotten hysterical with joy or fallen so in love that she'd lost her head.

Until she'd met Kenzie.

Pausing with her toothbrush buzzing away in place in her mouth, she let herself remember their first meeting, on a bus tour to Lake Mead and Hoover Dam. As she'd stepped onto the bus, she'd immediately spotted Kenzie, sitting by herself and staring out the window. Something about her profile had made Saana's heart stutter, and she'd slowed, her gaze affixed to the beautiful, dark-skinned woman, willing her to look up. As she got closer, she'd noticed the plaid shirt, worn like a loose jacket over a black tee but unable to fully disguise the lush figure beneath. Short, curly hair stuck out from beneath a ballcap, and as Saana paused beside the seat, she could see the smooth skin of one thigh between the rips in Kenzie's jeans.

Even her well-worn cowboy boots caused Saana's instant fascination to increase.

Then those gorgeous, umber eyes had turned her way, and Saana's knees weakened.

Hanging on to her cool by a thread, she'd smiled and asked, "Anyone sitting here?"

Kenzie had blinked up at her for what seemed like forever and then smiled back, sending Saana's heart rate through the roof.

"I guess you are."

Saana had thought of that moment often, classifying it as love at first sight. *Un coup de foudre*, as her French teacher called it. Something Saana had never believed in.

Until that first glimpse of Kenzie.

All she'd wanted when she went to Vegas was a simple holiday. One that wasn't on the Riviera or anywhere that would necessitate evening gowns and meetups with old school friends or relatives. The stress she'd been under in getting her practice ready to open had been enormous, and she'd known once she opened the doors, she would only get busier.

Having a quickie romance hadn't even been on her radar. Falling in love? If someone had mentioned that, she'd have laughed herself silly.

But didn't love last forever instead of dying, leaving only anger behind?

And, if she were being honest, lust.

Kenzie had been the best lover she'd ever had, and even now, angrier than before, remembering the things they'd done together drove shards of arousal deep into Saana's body.

Finished in the bathroom, she went to her closet to pull out a sundress. After she tugged it on, she crossed the room to the windows and, once there, opened the curtains facing the pool house. It was attached to the main house by an enclosed walkway and was sometimes used to house guests, as well as all the paraphernalia needed for days on or by the water.

The blinds were drawn, and there was no sign of life.

Had Kenzie left already?

Saana was about check the security feed to see if her car was still parked out front when the door to the pool house opened, and Kenzie stepped out into the early-morning light.

A shiver climbed Saana's spine as she watched her estranged wife walk down the path, through the flower garden and to the dock. Kenzie was wearing her usual casual attire, which consisted of colorful board shorts with a plain white T-shirt that hung down to her hips and rubber flip-flops on her feet. She hadn't taken off the satin sleep bonnet she wore to stop her hair from getting tangled, which brought back another rush of memories and made Saana smile despite herself. For a moment, rage slipped away, leaving her to savor Kenzie's confident stride, the roll of her hips, the straight-backed posture that silently proclaimed that she was a force to be reckoned with.

And she was that—an immovable force. Independent to a fault, despite her easygoing nature. Determined. Self-reliant.

All this, Saana had learned quickly during their first few days together as spouses, which made Kenzie's plea for help that much more powerful.

Yet it was impossible to disregard the past, especially in light of not being able to understand it. There had been no closure—no proper explanation. Saana had tried to give Kenzie whatever—everything—she could possibly want or need, and yet it hadn't been enough. Instead, she'd been left feeling as though she'd failed— a sensation Saana wasn't used to and hated with every cell in her body.

It was impossible to put the pain aside, but something deep inside whispered that she was being hypocritical. She, who constantly talked about helping others, was turning her back on someone desperate enough to put her considerable pride and independence aside to ask for her assistance.

The person Saana had loved with every fiber of her being.

Already, despite her bone-deep resistance to the ramifications, a plan was forming in her head, and for the first time in her life, she cursed her habitually methodical nature. It laid itself out before her, presenting itself as the most natural thing in the world. She would help Kenzie the way she'd asked and perhaps, in so doing, might at least be able to put a period on this painful, distressing part of her life.

Yet there were numerous stumbling blocks, she thought, watching her wife sit on one of the benches overlooking the water and rub the small of her back as if it ached. The one thing Kenzie valued above all else was her autonomy, and if she accepted Saana's conditions, she'd have to surrender it—lock, stock and barrel.

And Saana herself would have to keep the tightest control ever on her own emotions. There could be no sliding back into a real relationship. The reminder that once Kenzie got what she wanted she'd leave again had to be kept at the forefront constantly.

Saana knew herself well enough to admit that, given the slightest chance, she'd fall for her enigmatic, frustrating, absolutely wonderful wife all over again.

Turning away from the window, she went to finish getting ready, already regretting the impulse to help. Caught somewhere between hoping Kenzie refused that help and longing for another chance to spend time with the woman who'd captured her heart.

* * *

Kenzie sat on one of the benches near the dock, looking out over the water, still trying unsuccessfully to figure out what to do next.

Return to San Antonio?

Stay in Florida?

Take off and start over somewhere else, hoping the Beauchamps wouldn't find her? Maybe head south to Mexico since she was fluent in Spanish? Her savings would definitely go further there.

She had no idea what would be best, but she did know coming here had been a terrible mistake.

Returning to the house in Indialantic had brought back all those feelings of inadequacy she'd run from before, and she despised herself for it. No matter how out of place she'd always felt here, this was no time to be dwelling on it.

Everything she did from now on had to be in the twins' best interests, and if Saana had agreed to her crazy plan, Kenzie would have had to just suck it up.

But Saana had turned her down flat, so she could go on hating the house as much as she wanted.

Not that it was ugly or a monstrosity, despite Kenzie's habit of thinking of it as a mausoleum. In fact, the rambling two-story structure, built in a vaguely Spanish style, with its elaborate gardens and massive pool in the back, was probably someone's dream home. Especially being set on a two-acre riverside lot—almost unheard of in this small enclave—and having a private dock and boathouse.

But she'd felt lost and insignificant in the house, particularly when Saana was out and Kenzie was there alone, which happened often in those early days. The great room was twice as big as the entire downstairs of the house Kenzie had grown up in, and it was just one of three sitting rooms on the ground floor. And there was also a formal dining room, a breakfast room, a large library and office, and a room Saana referred to as *the parlor*.

Kenzie could agree that, viewed from the angle of a disinterested outsider, it was palatial, if old-fashioned and far too big. One weekend afternoon, while they were swimming, she'd asked Saana why she lived here, and her reply had been enlightening.

"My grandfather left it to me," she'd said with unmistakable fondness in her voice. "Under his will, Gran had a life interest in the house, but she moved to Palm Beach right after he died, so I moved in."

"Don't you find it too big?" Kenzie had asked, really meaning that she thought it too huge for just the two of them, but Saana had shaken her head, obviously not hearing the subtext.

"It's my family home," she'd replied, moving

closer to Kenzie in the water until her hands brushed against Kenzie's thighs. "My mother was raised here, and I spent a lot of time with my grandparents when I was growing up, so it holds wonderful memories for me."

Then she'd grinned. "Besides, it's a historic house, built in the 1940s by a Hollywood producer as a place to entertain movie stars. Can you imagine what they got up to down here? All the crazy parties they must have had, far from the prying eyes of the press?"

"All the orgies, you mean?" Kenzie had asked, completely distracted by the sight of Saana's lovely breasts bobbing just below the waterline, barely covered by her skimpy bikini top. "All the skinny-dipping and naughtiness… Like this?"

She'd been untying Saana's top as she spoke, and her wife's shuddering sigh of agreement had been more than enough for her to let the conversation fade away.

Okay, those memories weren't helpful right now. They made her want to squirm with the ever-present desire for Saana—that inescapable current of arousal that flowed in Kenzie's blood for her, no matter how far apart they were.

They were perfectly matched between the sheets. Unfortunately, that harmony hadn't existed outside the bedroom.

Besides, that was all in the past. Right now,

what she needed to do was concentrate on the present and, most importantly, the future.

The sound of a door closing had her looking over her shoulder, and her heart gave a shudder at the sight of Saana walking down the path toward her. Dressed in a vividly patterned dress that hugged her breasts and flowed like water around her lithe figure, she made Kenzie's mouth water and a burning lump form in her stomach.

No matter how hard she'd tried, she hadn't been able to forget.

Not just the way it felt to make love with Saana but what it felt like to love and be loved.

The tenderness.

The sensation of having someone to care for and knowing Saana had cared about her too.

She knew she'd never experience anything like it again because she'd given her entire being over into Saana's hands, and there was no getting it back.

But she couldn't let the other woman know the effect she still had, so from somewhere deep inside, she found the ability to appear calm and unconcerned as Saana got closer. She even tore her gaze away and turned back toward the water.

"You always loved it down here," Saana said as she took a seat on the other bench. "I figured this is where you'd be. We need to talk."

There was something different about the way she spoke. Her tone was still cool, but also, beneath the control, there was a hint of something else. Not hesitancy but maybe close to it.

"I plan to leave soon," Kenzie said, unwilling to explain that she didn't have the first clue about where to go. "So don't worry that I'll be hanging around too much longer."

"Actually, I came to tell you that I'm reconsidering your request."

Kenzie's head whipped around, seemingly of its own free will, so she could see Saana's expressionless face. Her heart stopped for an instant before galloping back into action, and her breath hung suspended in her chest long enough to make her light-headed.

Finally forcing her lungs to work again, she stammered, "Wh…what?"

Saana shrugged, coolly dismissive.

"I've decided to help you after all. But there is a number of important conditions you have to agree to."

The surge of excitement that had roared through Kenzie waned slightly at Saana's words, replaced by suspicion laced with an undercurrent of fear, although she wasn't sure what she was afraid of.

Swallowing that dread, reminding herself this was the best outcome she could hope for, she licked her bottom lip and asked, "Like what?"

"The first is that no one, and I mean no one, can know what we're doing. Our subterfuge must be completely and utterly believable to any on-lookers."

Kenzie ran her tongue over her suddenly dry lips, trying to think through the consequences of Saana's words.

"Did you have anyone in particular in mind?" she asked.

Saana's nostrils flared slightly as she drew in a sharp breath. "My family. Delores."

"But shouldn't they know the truth?"

How on earth could they keep the true nature of their relationship from people so close to Saana? Delores, her housekeeper, was at the house every weekday. Keeping up the facade of a happy marriage in front of her would be almost impossible.

"They are the *last* people who should," Saana said, the steel in her voice unmistakable. "Think about it. If the case against you goes to court and they are called to testify, are you expecting them to perjure themselves for you?"

If she were being honest, Kenzie knew she would ask just that, in a heartbeat, but she could see Saana's point. So, reluctantly, she agreed. "You're right."

It struck her, then, that she would be giving up her autonomy to Saana again, and it wasn't in her nature to give over control of her life so easily.

"I'll need to work," she said quickly, wanting Saana to know she didn't intend to sponge off her just because she was in a bind. "I have to think about the future, and that means not sitting around for however long it takes to get the legalities cleared up."

There was a long pause as Saana's gaze searched hers until Kenzie was fighting the urge to look away. Then another of those careless shrugs.

"I know of a clinic that needs a nurse right away. I can put you in touch with the HR lady on Monday, if you want."

"Yes." She knew it was petty to add neither *please* nor *thank you* to the acceptance, but although she'd been the one to request the assistance, having to accept it made her hackles rise. "That would be great."

After another long look, the corners of Saana's lips twisted, and she got up.

"I'll take care of it, but now I have somewhere to be. While I'm gone, there's plenty of food in the kitchen, so make yourself at home."

Her mouth twisted again, and Kenzie bit her lip as the unintentional barb hit her straight in the solar plexus.

Or *was* it unintentional? From Saana's expression, it seemed that way, but Kenzie was having a hard time reading her.

Before she could answer, Saana continued. "We'll discuss the situation further when I get home this afternoon. You should take your bags up to the bedroom and start getting settled in."

Again, Kenzie found her breath caught in her throat, trapping whatever she was going to say next, as the full truth of what she'd agreed to exploded in her brain.

"The bedroom," she parroted like an idiot, waves of heat and cold running uncontrollably over her skin.

That gained her a haughty, eyebrows-raised glance from Saana.

"How else will we convince everyone that we're back together if we're not sharing my bed?" Saana asked before turning and walking away.

CHAPTER FIVE

HOW LIKE SAANA to simply carry on with her life as if nothing unusual had happened, making an earth-shattering pronouncement, then leaving Kenzie reeling in her wake.

What could be more important than sticking around and hashing out the situation now that she'd decided to help?

However, it didn't surprise Kenzie that her wife had dropped a bombshell and left, sticking to her schedule no matter what. Saana lived an almost regimented life. Nothing could be allowed to interfere with her plans. Oh, she could be spontaneous on occasion, but once she'd come up with an agenda, it was written in stone.

Which always made Kenzie want to mess those plans up.

But as she watched Saana go back into the house, Kenzie faced the agonizing fact that her wife was right. While Saana was close to her parents and brother, back in the day there hadn't been a lot of family get-togethers. Unless that had changed, the Ameris weren't Kenzie's biggest problem. Delores would be the hardest to fool since the housekeeper came Monday to Friday, arriving about ten in the morning and leaving at four in the afternoon.

She'd not only potentially see Saana and Kenzie interacting, but she'd also see all the little signs of how they lived. Whether one bed had been slept in or two. Where Kenzie had her clothes hanging or if one of the myriad guest bathrooms had been used.

There was no way to get around Delores.

A familiar oily sensation suddenly arose in the back of her throat, bringing Kenzie out of her unhappy thoughts. Looking down at her stomach, rubbing it with both hands, she dredged up a smile from somewhere.

"You guys are hungry, huh? Yeah, Momma's been neglectin' you, but we'll go rustle up some grub now, just to keep you happy."

After getting up, she made her way toward the mansion slowly, wondering if Saana was still there or had already left.

And she couldn't help the feeling of mingled annoyance and relief when she heard Saana's car start up and then drive away.

As she ate, Kenzie tried to figure out some way to keep up the pretense of the marriage being back on the right track without sharing a bed.

The last thing she needed was to be that close to Saana.

The need to touch, to arouse, to feel that lithe, sexy body coming apart beneath her hands and lips might well pound all her good sense to dust.

There must be some way to make their lies believable without getting all tangled up together that way again.

From the beginning, they'd been unable to keep their hands off each other. They'd actually slept together the day after they met, and if Kenzie had had her way, it would have happened the first day instead. But she'd realized right off the bat that Saana wouldn't want to be rushed. She'd thought Saana wasn't as comfortable with physical intimacy as Kenzie was, but that reserve, near hesitancy, had made her even more attractive.

And when they'd finally gotten into bed together…

The deep shudder that fired through her body had Kenzie shutting those memories down and pushing her plate away.

She had to forget the past and concentrate on the present and future. Her babies were depending on her, and right now, she needed to figure out the best way to make the situation with Saana work without making everything worse.

Maybe they could negotiate once Saana decided to get her behind back to the mansion and discuss it, but in the meantime, Kenzie accepted what she had to do.

After bringing her car around to the garage, she pulled out her bags. For the first time, she was glad there was an elevator in the house, which she'd silently scoffed at before.

"Did your grandparents have mobility issues?" she'd asked Saana when she first saw it.

"No," she'd replied with a chuckle. "It was put in when the house was built, back in the forties. Apparently, no one wanted to climb stairs if they could ride up instead."

And it was so elaborate, with gold paint all over everything, including the carved woodwork and the folding grill at the front.

Ridiculous but useful now, when she had a couple of hefty suitcases and a pair of babies in her belly that caused her to think—and over-think—everything she did. While the doctor had told her she was healthy and shouldn't change her lifestyle, it was impossible not to worry.

These babies were precious and, in her mind, a miracle. Kenzie would do everything in her power to keep them safe and bring them into the world as strong as possible.

At the door to Saana's room, Kenzie's breath hitched, and she found herself rooted in place, battered by memories—both good and bad.

The room looked the same. Large and bright, it was decorated with sleek furniture and soothing colors. But Kenzie felt anything but relaxed as her gaze tracked from the bed to the chaise longue, then the dressing table, each bringing to mind a moment of past tenderness or passion. There, in front of the fireplace, they'd lain with entangled legs and caressing hands, whispers of love barely audible above the crackle of the flames.

Wandering in, Kenzie blinked against the tears filling her eyes. She'd stood behind Saana at the vanity, brushing her hair, which then had fallen halfway down her back. Watched with sweet delight the way her wife's eyes had drifted closed in pleasure.

There was even a lingering scent that was fundamentally Saana, and each time Kenzie inhaled it was like taking a little of their past back into herself.

It was heartbreaking and enticing all at once, and Kenzie knew she shouldn't indulge in this soppy emotionality.

Giving herself a mental shake, she quickly unpacked, placing her clothes in the ample walk-in closet, and then high-tailed it out of the room and back downstairs. Once there, though, the weight of the house seemed to press down on her, and the anger she'd felt toward Saana earlier returned.

Why should she stick around, cooling her jets while Saana was off doing whatever?

And wouldn't it serve Saana right to come home and not find Kenzie waiting like she expected?

With a toss of her head, Kenzie went back upstairs to change. Then, without any real idea of where she was going, she locked up the house and took off.

Driving south, she ended up at the Sebastian Inlet State Park and, after stopping at the commissary to buy a couple bottles of water, went for a long walk on the beach, followed by lunch at the beachside restaurant.

Determined not to be at the mansion when Saana got home, she took her time meandering north on Highway A1A later that afternoon, stopping here and there, reorienting herself. In the past, she'd been so wrapped up with Saana and her studies she hadn't really explored as much as she could have.

Yet she knew she was really just dragging her feet in the hopes that Saana would get home and, finding her gone, realize Kenzie wasn't sitting around waiting for her.

The joke was on her, though, when she returned to Indialantic after having dinner and Saana wasn't there. Eventually, when the exhaustion brought on by her travels and day out was overwhelming, she admitted defeat and went to bed, fuming.

The next morning, when she realized Saana

hadn't come home at all, she was forced to face a thought that hadn't even occurred to her before.

Was there someone else in Saana's life? Someone she'd run to, so as to get away from Kenzie?

And the rush of jealousy was both unwanted and far too strong to be ignored.

Saana woke up, disoriented, to find her cheek on something hard, her arms above her head on the same flat surface. It was only when she straightened, groaning at the pain in her neck and back, that she realized she'd fallen asleep at her desk. For a long moment, she couldn't understand why she was in her Suntree clinic office; then it all came rushing back.

Kenzie was in Florida, at the house.

Pregnant and wanting help.

Saana shook her head, rubbing her sore cheek, as she acknowledged that she'd run away yesterday, scared by what she was agreeing to, what it would do to her emotional equilibrium.

But she'd spent the whole day before trying to figure out another way to help Kenzie without her staying in Florida—at the Indialantic house—and had come up empty.

And she was honest enough to recognize that she didn't really want to find an alternative. That there was a huge part of her that reveled in the thought of being around Kenzie again. Having her back in her life.

She must be a secret masochist. Hadn't the past pain taught her anything?

When Kenzie had said she was going back to Texas for an undetermined period of time to take care of her sick aunt, Saana tried to find some other way to solve the problem.

"I can hire a nurse to take care of her," she'd told Kenzie. "Or we can find a really nice long-term care facility."

"Aunt Lena doesn't need either of those things yet." Kenzie had hardly seemed to be listening, intent on her packing. "What she needs is someone to be there with her. Someone she knows and trusts."

"What about her children?" Saana had heard the desperation in her own voice and despised herself for it. "Why aren't they taking care of her? They live in San Antonio, don't they?"

Kenzie had just shaken her head, rejecting every suggestion, refusing to say how long she'd be gone.

"Listen, with the pandemic, both Raul and Justin have formed a bubble with their families, and Ashley's as useful to her mom as teats on a bull. I *have* to go."

And she'd refused to say she'd come back at some point.

Saana had seen it as another example of her wife's stubbornness and overreaching independence. Her aunt was her responsibility, and she wouldn't consider any ideas other than what she'd come up with, even if it meant abandoning her marriage.

Abandoning Saana, who loved her beyond reason.

And there was no getting around the fact that this was, once again, a temporary situation. Once Kenzie got custody of her babies, she'd take off.

That was what Saana had to keep front of mind, no matter how her silly heart was already trying to get involved.

A quick glance at the clock showed it was just after six, giving her ample time to get home and back to the office in time for her first appointment at nine.

There was a lot she had to do today, along with her usual clinic appointments, and the first would be talking to Kenzie.

Had she wondered where Saana had spent the night? Had she slept in their bed, the way Saana had told her she needed to?

Saana forced herself to shrug at the idea and ignore the wash of heat climbing her spine.

Just because they'd be sharing a bed didn't mean this bone-deep longing would—or should—be assuaged. In fact, making love with Kenzie would be the very worst thing she could do.

Things were complicated enough, she thought as she headed out into the already bright morning light, without throwing any more knots into the puzzle.

Hopefully, the HR manager at the Eau Gallie clinic would get her message first thing this morning and contact Kenzie regarding the job there.

Saana stopped as she was driving out of the parking lot.

Did Kenzie still have the same number? She hadn't thought to ask. Hitting the button on the steering wheel, she recorded a text message.

Is this still your phone number, McKenzie?

Then, without waiting for a reply, she headed for home, running through everything she wanted to get done over the next couple of days.

If she could keep thinking about the practicalities, she would be okay.

Hopefully.

It took twenty minutes to get home, during which Saana sent a slew of text messages, trying to get life into some semblance of order. There was nothing worse than feeling as though things were topsy-turvy, and with Kenzie's sudden return, she needed everything else to be under control.

Just as she was approaching the gates, her phone pinged with a one-word reply from Kenzie:

Yes.

Kenzie at her laconic best, and it put Saana on alert. You knew there was trouble on the horizon when Kenzie became quiet instead of her usual easy, slightly chatty self.

It caused Saana to be ready for some type of battle when she entered the house through the garage and followed the sound of the kitchen radio playing.

Although her back was turned and she was chopping something on the counter in front of her, as soon as Saana stepped into the kitchen, Kenzie said, "Mornin'. Want some breakfast?"

Not quite what she was expecting, so it took Saana a moment to catch up and reply. "Yes, please. I have to get ready for work, though."

"No problem. I haven't started cooking yet. How long will you be?"

"About twenty minutes?"

She made it a question and got a wave of Kenzie's knife hand in reply. "That'll work."

Feeling dismissed, Saana headed upstairs to shower. By the time she came back, breakfast was on the table, and they both started eating.

"Mmm…" Saana closed her eyes for a moment in pleasure as the flavor of the egg white, spinach and cheese omelet burst on her tongue. "This is so good. Thank you."

Kenzie gave a nod, acknowledging the compliment, but Saana saw a flash of amusement cross her face.

Suddenly, it was easy to read Kenzie again, and Saana remembered a conversation they'd had before, when Kenzie had realized Saana didn't know how to cook.

"How do you get to thirty-two without being able to cook?" she'd asked, laughing but with raised eyebrows that hinted at her horror. "I was in charge of making dinner at Aunt Lena's since I was eight or nine."

It had been one more reminder of just how different their upbringings had been and the responsibility Kenzie had shouldered at a young age. Not wanting to show how touched and saddened she felt at this glimpse of her wife's previous life, she'd given a dismissive shrug.

"I never had to learn and wasn't very interested anyway."

It had made her want to do everything for Kenzie. Wrap her in cotton wool and give her any and everything she'd had to do without.

Well, that wasn't in the cards anymore, and she wasn't planning to even pretend she still wanted to cosset Kenzie.

Clearing her throat, she banished those thoughts and got back to practicalities. "You'll need an ob-gyn here. I can give you a list of the best ones, and you can see if any of them will take you as a patient."

Kenzie hesitated and then lifted her chin a notch. "I was going to ask you if you could get me in with whichever one you thought would be best for me, in my situation. If I just call and ask if he or she is taking new patients, I might get turned down."

It was hard to keep her instinctive reaction of shock off her face, but Saana thought she did a good job of it.

"I can do that, if that's what you want."

"It is," Kenzie replied, her chin still at a combative angle. "I want the best for the babies."

Apparently, there was nothing Kenzie wouldn't do for those babies—even ask for more help.

"I'll reach out to Dr. Ramcharam," she replied. "She's the best in my book, and a maternal-fetal medicine specialist too." She glanced at her phone, then pushed back from the table. "I have to go. My first patient is at nine."

"So I guess you don't have time to talk now?" The question was mild enough, but Saana wasn't fooled. The crease that appeared in Kenzie's forehead told the true story.

"No, I have to get to work."

"What do I say to Delores? Do I just brazen it out?" No mistaking the hint of temper in her voice. "We haven't even decided what we're going to tell everyone."

Battling a rush of unaccountable anger, Saana shrugged.

"You figure it out," she replied, hearing the frost in her own voice but unable to suppress it. "All I told everyone was that you had gone to nurse your aunt, who had terminal pancreatic cancer. Just let me know what you decide our story is going to be."

She'd been hopeful at first that Kenzie would come back. Then hope had turned to sorrow, which had to be hidden so no one would feel sorry for her. Afterward, she'd simply felt embarrassed at having made a fool of herself over a woman who clearly didn't love her the way she'd claimed.

Angry as she thought about all she'd been put through by the beautiful woman across the table from her, she walked away before she could say something she might regret. But she was brought to a halt at the door by Kenzie's voice.

"One last thing. Are you seeing anyone? Because, if you are, I'll find some other way to deal with the situation."

How tempting it was to lie and say she was. It would be the perfect out, wouldn't it?

"No. I'm not seeing anyone right now."

And she didn't wait for Kenzie to reply.

CHAPTER SIX

KENZIE TURNED IN to the parking lot at the Eau Gallie clinic twenty minutes early and looked around. Just a block away from US 1, the area was mixed residential and commercial, although the majority of the businesses seemed to have failed, since the buildings she could see were mostly abandoned. The few remaining houses looked sad and unloved, some with boarded-up windows and overgrown yards.

The clinic itself was housed in what looked like an old strip mall, and that, at least, looked clean and well maintained. The sign above the door was fairly small and simply said *Preston Medical*, and inside she could see a figure standing by the door. It looked like a guard.

Tilting the rearview mirror, she checked her face and hair and then sat back in her seat and took a deep breath.

She hadn't felt this frazzled in a long time. And while she'd be the first to admit life had been throwing a lot of stuff at her over the past ten months, she placed the blame squarely at Saana's feet.

Once faced with the situation they were now in, the Saana of old would've put together a plan and presented it as being written in stone. Her way or the highway. Now it seemed she was leaving it all up to Kenzie to sort out. Not that Kenzie was quarreling about that. After all, it was what she was used to from everyone else in her life.

Just not Saana, who was hardwired to take control of any situation involving someone she cared about. Methodically plan everything within her ability and do whatever it took to make that plan work. Abdicating the responsibility of figuring out what they should say demonstrated just how little she cared—Saana was no longer in love. It explained everything.

Which should be a good thing, right? They both knew their impulsive marriage had been a mistake and that it wouldn't have lasted, even if Kenzie hadn't gone back to Texas to take care of Aunt Lena.

It was better this way, especially for Saana, but it still hurt like hell.

Not that she was looking to revive their marriage, Kenzie reminded herself sternly. All that was important was to put on a good performance for the courts and have them decide in her favor.

That was what had galvanized her earlier to get their story straight since Saana hadn't.

The best thing, she decided, was to keep it simple and just add a few details so it all made sense. She'd texted Saana the concocted story, asking if she had anything to add, and gotten one word in response.

No.

Thankfully, the call from Marion Nunez, the HR lady at Preston Medical, had come at nine. Setting the appointment for ten thirty gave Kenzie an opportunity to get out of the house before Delores got to work.

She hadn't felt competent to deal with the housekeeper just then.

Now, with another glance at the time, she decided to go in.

The man inside opened the door as soon as she got to it, asking her name and checking the clipboard before stepping back so she could fully enter the waiting area. Then he called Ms. Nunez to let her know Kenzie was there, and within a couple of minutes, a short, older woman with bright pink hair came bustling into the reception area.

"Ah, McKenzie," she said with a broad smile. "It's so nice to meet you. Thank you for coming on such short notice."

"My pleasure," she replied, shaking the outstretched hand.

"Come on, then. Follow me, and we'll have a chat."

The HR office was to the left, down a corridor, past some examination rooms and a couple of doors with brackets on them, clearly to hold signs of some type. Once they were seated on either side of Ms. Nunez's desk, Kenzie found herself the focus of the other woman's sharp blue gaze.

"I was looking over your CV before you came and was interested by the fact that you've only been qualified for two years. Can you tell me about your path to nursing?"

Ouch. She was going straight to the weak spot in the CV, and Kenzie felt her heart sink even as she kept the smile on her face.

"Well, ma'am, I always knew I wanted to be a nurse but also knew I'd have to keep workin' while I studied so as not to be in debt when I left college. So it took me longer than most to get my degree. As you can see, I did work as a nurses' assistant at the hospital before I qualified, and that experience has been invaluable."

Ms. Nunez nodded seemingly happy with the explanation. "I do see that, and it's telling that the same hospital you worked at before immediately hired you on after you graduated." She steepled her fingers under her chin. "You were told that, if hired, this would be a temporary position?"

"That's all I'm looking for at this time." Kenzie knew it was against labor laws for the other woman to ask if she was pregnant, but she didn't offer that information either. She really wanted something to do, to make money, until the babies arrived. There was no way she'd give them a reason not to hire her.

"Good." Seemingly satisfied, Ms. Nunez leaned back in her chair. "Let me tell you a little about the clinic and the work we do here."

Kenzie had looked it up online while she was getting dressed to come to the interview, and she knew about the Preston Trust and the fact that it was a low-cost facility, but Ms. Nunez was able to tell her a great deal more.

"We treat women who've been referred to us by shelters, other clinics, emergency rooms, etcetera, but our goal is not just to treat immediate wounds or issues but develop a care plan for the patients. To this end, we partner with labs, specialists and pharmacies to ensure a holistic approach."

She paused, making sure Kenzie was following, and after receiving a nod, continued.

"We have a radiologist, endocrinologist and ob-gyn on-site once a month, offering mammograms, diabetes clinics and pelvic exams. But the mainstay of our clinic is the nurses, who are charged not only with assisting the doctors, but are also our eyes and ears when it comes to patient needs. The directors believe that the only way to truly serve the community is to allow the women coming here to express their needs. To become, in effect, stakeholders in the clinic."

"I understand," Kenzie said slowly. "I grew up in a poor neighborhood when I was a child, and people there often used the emergency room as their primary care facility. A place like this would allow more women to have their medical needs met without clogging up emerge."

"Exactly." Ms. Nunez smiled and then, totally unexpectedly, added, "Can you start tomorrow afternoon?"

Caught off guard, Kenzie could only stare like a deer caught in the headlights and grin like a fool.

"Yes. Yes, I can," she finally said, causing Ms. Nunez to lightly slap her hands on her desk and push to her feet.

"Perfect. Let me show you around."

An hour later, Kenzie left, feeling as if she were walking on air. She'd been hopeful about the job but hadn't dreamed she'd be hired on immediately. And this was exactly the type of facility she'd have picked to work at. Not only was it set up to do good for women in need, but also it operated during the afternoon and evening. Saana worked during the day, while Kenzie would be working at night, thereby limiting the amount of time they spent together.

A win all round.

Just as she settled into the driver's seat, still grinning, her phone rang.

Speak of the devil.

"Hi, Saana. What's up?"

"Just checking to see if you heard from the people at the clinic yet."

Kenzie couldn't hold back the little bubble of laughter that rose in her throat. "I just finished the interview. I start tomorrow."

"Congratulations. You can tell me all about it later, before we go to my parents for dinner."

"What?"

"No need to shriek in my ear." Having just about caused Kenzie's heart to stop, Saana had the audacity to sound amused. "We're going to have to face them sooner rather than later. I called Mom and told her you were back, and she invited us over. They're expecting us at six-thirty."

"I was hoping for later rather than sooner," Kenzie muttered. "But will you be back from work in time to get there?" In the past, Saana had often worked until eight or nine at night.

"Yes, but tonight's the only night I can, so we have to go. See you at the house at about five. Bye."

Kenzie cursed under her breath and stared at the phone for a moment more before tossing it on the passenger seat.

It was too much for one day. Clearly in agreement, one of the babies rolled over, making Kenzie gasp and rub the spot where a little elbow—or was that a foot?—poked out from her side.

"Yes," she crooned, kneading the little bump. "You agree, right? Getting all dressed up to go see the Ameris isn't high on our list of fun things to do."

Although she had to admit Saana's parents had never been mean to her or made her feel unwelcome. What they *had* made her feel was like a country bumpkin. Not by anything they said but simply by being their habitual, elegant selves.

Speaking of which...

"What the heck am I supposed to wear?"

Nothing she had from when she lived here before would fit, and just the thought of driving to one of the elegant boutiques in Viera to look for something was exhausting. Looking back at the early days of their marriage, she recognized her own desperation to fit in, to not embarrass Saana, and she kissed her teeth in annoyance.

Reality now was, they were playing at being together for the babies' sakes, and Kenzie no longer felt the need to bend over backward to pretend she belonged. She never would, and that, in its own way, was freeing.

They could take her as she was.

But that didn't mean she could turn up at Saana's parents' home in a T-shirt and board shorts or the scrubs she'd worn to the interview.

"We're goin' shopping, babies. But don't worry," she added, starting the car, "it won't take too long. I promise."

* * *

Of course the one day she absolutely needed to leave work on time, Saana found herself running late with a patient, not getting home until almost five forty-five.

"I won't be long," she called to Kenzie, who was in the small TV room off the great room.

The only answer she got sounded suspiciously like a snort, but she didn't have time to investigate.

After a quick shower and having gotten dressed, she hurried back downstairs, calling, "I'm ready."

The TV went off, and Saana heard the distinctive clack of cowboy boots approaching.

"You're gonna be late for your own funeral," Kenzie drawled as she came down the hallway, her tone light but her chin tilted up at a pugnacious angle.

She was dressed in jeans and cowboy boots but had on a soft cotton short-sleeved tunic in swirls of greens, blues and copper that clung to her breasts. Then it furled softly down over her belly to her hips. Her hair was a riot of twisted curls around her head, framing her face, and she'd added a simple pair of copper-toned earrings and a chunky bead necklace that nettled right in her cleavage.

Saana's breath caught in her throat, and for a moment, she couldn't speak. Couldn't move.

And her heart was racing so hard her entire body flashed hot.

Molten.

Like wax dripping from an upended candle.

Kenzie came to a halt in front of her, eyes flashing, chin still at that combative angle, but Saana didn't have the presence of mind to understand what the problem possibly could be.

Instead, instinctively, she blurted, "You look amazing."

Kenzie's lips parted as though she were about to speak, hung open for a second and then snapped shut again.

Shaking her head, she brushed past Saana and muttered, "Thanks. You look nice, too, as usual. Now, let's go. We're gonna be late."

Why was it so hard to get her legs to move? She all but stumbled after Kenzie to the car, trying—and failing—to keep her gaze off the swing of the other woman's hips.

By the time they got going, Saana's mouth was as dry as sawdust and her brain was a whirligig.

"What did you tell your parents?"

Kenzie's question forced Saana to pull herself together, but she had to moisten her lips before she could speak.

"What you suggested: That before your aunt passed away, you'd been asked to be surrogate for your cousin. We talked about it and I didn't have a problem, and you planned to come home as soon after giving birth as possible. Then, when your cousin didn't want the babies, we decided to keep them ourselves."

Kenzie didn't answer immediately, and when Saana glanced over at her, she had her chin on her hand and was looking out the side mirror.

Then she sighed.

"I want you to know I'm really grateful for your help. I know I'm causing you all kinds of trouble—"

Unable to bear it, Saana cut her off.

"It's fine. Really." A lie, but told in her own best interests. No way she'd let Kenzie know just how much having her around again was playing havoc with her senses. "I can understand your need to protect your babies, and I said I'd help, and I will."

"Yes." Kenzie sighed again, but quietly, probably hoping Saana wouldn't hear it. "I do know how committed you are once you make a decision."

Saana waited to hear what else she'd say, but Kenzie fell silent and stayed that way all the way to the Merritt Island estate.

As they walked toward the entrance to the house, Kenzie stuck her hands under her tunic and swiped them down the sides of her jeans. Saana tried to ignore the tender sensation the gesture caused to bloom in her chest but couldn't.

Reaching out, she snagged Kenzie's hand

and laced their fingers together. When the other woman stiffened, Saana squeezed gently.

"We're supposed to present a united front," she murmured. "Remember?"

And Kenzie shook her shoulders, as if to loosen up tight muscles.

"Sure," she replied just as the front door opened, revealing Mom and Dad waiting for them.

Saana really hadn't been sure what reception to expect from her parents, but immediately, when they stepped into the foyer, she knew it was going to be all right.

"McKenzie," Mom said, her welcome obvious as she pulled Kenzie in for a hug. "It's so good to have you back. I'm so sorry to hear about your aunt."

"Thank you, Mrs. A."

"But now we have so much to look forward to! Twins on the way? Do you know what you're having?"

The shock of hearing her mother say *we* made Saana freeze, and then she was horrified to realize she hadn't even thought to ask the sex of the babies.

"Oh," Kenzie said, smiling, although Saana could see signs of strain around her eyes. "At least one boy—but each time they do an ultrasound, the other baby is hidin' the naughty parts, so I'm not sure what the final outcome will be."

"Surprises are always good," Mom replied with a laugh. Her hands were hovering on either side of Kenzie's belly, not touching, but clearly longing to make contact.

Kenzie stiffened, her back arching just a little, and she gave a sharp inhale.

"Someone is turnin' somersaults in here," she said. Then, without hesitation, she reached out and took one of Mom's hands, placing it just to the left of her navel.

And Saana had to blink against tears at the sight of the two women joined together in that tender moment and the look of wonder and delight on her mother's face.

And later, when she finally went to bed, having given Kenzie a chance to fall asleep before she went upstairs, that was the image that followed her into sleep.

No wonder she awoke just as the sun was coming up and found herself spooning Kenzie from behind, her hand cupped around the sweet swell of the little lives within her womb.

Drowsy, good sense still lulled by sleep, she allowed herself to savor the scent and feel of the woman she'd always loved and the miracles she carried within.

Then Kenzie stirred, and reality intruded, causing Saana to roll away to her own side of the bed.

Into the emptiness.

CHAPTER SEVEN

THE FIRST DAY at a new job always brought butterflies to Kenzie's stomach, but when she got to the Preston Clinic for her first shift, she felt no nervousness at all. She was just glad to have something to do to take her out of the Indialantic mansion and help her not think about the muddle she'd created by coming back to Florida.

The guilt gnawing at her as she remembered Mrs. Ameri's excitement over the babies.

And she'd forgotten—or tried to forget—just how demonstrative Saana was in public. Touching Kenzie's hair, arm or leg as she talked. Even kissing her cheek as they sat on her parents' enclosed patio, watching the last rays of the sun disappear into night.

Not to mention the suppressed longing she'd felt when she'd woken up in Saana's arms this morning. Although Kenzie was the more demanding one in bed, Saana had always been the big spoon when they snuggled, and the sensation of being held that way once more had immediately ignited her desires.

Not just for sex but for love too. Lying there, Kenzie had found herself pretending everything was the way it used to be, and the urge to roll over and hold her wife tightly was almost impossible to resist.

It was too big, too much of a tangled mess, for her to contemplate right now, so it felt good to sign in for work and introduce herself to the head nurse, Minerva Hartley.

"Nice to meet you," Minerva said, giving Kenzie a firm handshake. "I know you got shown around before, but I'll show you where we keep the important stuff."

This was, of course, a more comprehensive and useful tour of the store cupboards, examination rooms and reporting system.

"We use an old-fashioned filing system," Minerva explained. "But everything gets entered into the computer by an outside firm." They were coming to the end of the tour, by the nurses' desk, and the clinic was about to open—patients were already filling the waiting room beyond the plexiglass barrier. "Each afternoon, you'll find your personal clipboard in your slot, and the front sheet will tell you which doctor you're assigned to for the shift."

As she spoke, Minerva pulled out a board and glanced at it.

"You're working with Dr. Ameri today."

"Ameri?"

It was impossible not to screech the name like a pup whose tail had been stepped on, and Minerva gave her a startled look.

"Yes. Dr. Saana Ameri. Do you know her?"

"Yes, we know each other."

The cool, controlled voice coming from behind her had Kenzie spinning around so quickly she stumbled, and an electric strike fired into her arm from where Saana steadied her.

Pulling away, she glared at her wife, who lifted an eyebrow in return.

"Is everything okay, Dr. Ameri?" Minerva asked, caught somewhere between caution and curiosity.

"Perfectly fine. I'll show McKenzie which rooms are ours, and then she can bring in our first patient."

With that, she turned on her heel and, after swiping her card, walked through the security door without checking to see if Kenzie was following.

"We'll be using exam rooms three and four," she said, once Kenzie had gotten herself under enough control to take off after her.

"What are you doing here?" Managing to keep her voice low enough not to be overheard was a struggle.

"I work here in the evenings," came the bland

reply, as if it should have been self-evident. Opening the door to the exam room, she waved Kenzie through. "Actually, since you'll probably eventually hear anyway, I was the one who set up this clinic."

Shocked, Kenzie found herself gaping at Saana and snapped her mouth shut. "You own it?"

Saana closed the door behind them and leaned against it.

"The Preston Trust owns and operates the practice, but I set up the trust." Kenzie tried to speak, but was cut off when Saana continued. "We don't have time to hash this out right now. There are patients waiting. You've been told what to do?"

That tone clearly said Saana was done talking, so, still steaming, Kenzie replied coolly, "Yes, Doctor."

But it took a moment for Saana to move from in front of the door, during which time they stared each other down. Even through her annoyance, Kenzie felt the pull of those gorgeous eyes and had to fight the urge to pull her wife close and kiss her senseless. Then Saana opened the door and stepped out, holding it for Kenzie to come through behind her and go call on the first patient.

Tearing her thoughts away from Saana and the bombshell she'd just dropped, Kenzie firmly put her mind on the upcoming shift. In comparison to working in a busy hospital urgent care clinic, the Preston Clinic was going to be a breeze as far as Kenzie was concerned, even if it meant being in constant contact with Saana. And the ability to interact more with the patients rather than rushing them in and out was a definite plus.

During the tour earlier, Minerva had explained, "We're expected to ask questions and advise the patients about the various services offered. Have they had a mammogram recently? Pelvic exam? Very often, at a doctor's office, patients are expected to only talk about the one issue they came in for, unless it's a yearly checkup. But many of these women don't have primary care, much less yearly exams, so it's up to us to mention these things. It allows them to think about it for a little while and not be taken by surprise when the doctor brings it up."

With all that in mind, Kenzie went to the waiting room and called her first patient, Miriam Durham. She was sixty-two, was complaining of extreme pain in her knees and had been referred to them by a community group specializing in assisting indigent members.

The lady, who came forward at a slow shuffle, had on what looked like several long-sleeved shirts, topped off with a knitted hoodie. Unusual in the Florida heat but not unheard of. Kenzie made a mental note to try to find out why Miriam was dressed that way. The answer could, to Saana, be important.

"Hi, Ms. Durham," she said as the patient finally got to her. "My name is Kenzie. If you'll come with me, I'll get your information, and then the doctor will be with you."

"Thanks, darlin'," the other woman said, shuffling alongside Kenzie into the back corridor.

At the general staging area, Kenzie said, "Let's just get your weight."

"Ugh." Miriam leaned heavily on Kenzie so as to step up onto the scale. "I don't even wanna know what I weigh now. It's just crept on over the last ten years and won't stop comin'. Guess I'm just at that time of life, huh?"

"Could be," Kenzie replied, noting the numbers on her chart and then helping Ms. Durham back down. "But it's something you should mention to the doctor when you see her."

"I planned to since I'm here about my poor knees. They hurt like the blazes, and I figured it might have something to do with my weight."

"When did you last have a full checkup?"

Miriam gave a rueful smile. "Chile, not since I left North Carolina about five years ago. With one thing and another, I just never had the chance. By the way, where're you from?"

"Texas." Kenzie opened the door to the examination room and steered Ms. Durham in.

"I thought I recognized that drawl," the older

lady said with a chuckle. "I followed a boy to Fort Hood when I was young. Married him too. First of my three marriages and probably the best, although it didn't last."

Kenzie laughed with her and then, after carefully helping her up onto the exam table, set about taking her blood pressure, oxygen-saturation level and pulse rate. The entire time, Miriam chatted about her three ex-husbands and her son, whom she said she'd come to Florida to be closer to.

"It's been hard, though," she said, no longer smiling. "His wife don't like having me around, and I hardly get to see my grandbabies. I lived with them for a little while when I first came here but eventually moved on because I was causin' trouble in the marriage, ya know? Like my momma used to say: two hens can't rule the same kitchen."

"I'm sorry to hear that." Kenzie patted Miriam's shoulder and then made a couple more notes on her chart. "Do you get to see him sometimes?"

"Yeah," Miriam said, but it was impossible not to hear the sadness in her voice or miss the gleam of tears in her eyes. "He brings Tia and Mikah to see me at a park near where I live, but only every now and then. It's hard to plan anything since I work shifts and he's busy all the time." She gave a little sniff. "I wish I could see them more—even look after them sometimes—but that can't work."

The door behind her opened just as Miriam added, "It's hard, being away from my grandbabies like that. They and my son are all I have left in the world."

"Hello, Ms. Durham. I'm Dr. Ameri."

The sound of Saana's voice, the brush of her shoulder as she stepped past, made a hard shiver fire along Kenzie's spine. Instinctively, she stepped back and held out the clipboard for Saana to take.

"Thank you, McKenzie."

There was no mistaking the dismissal in her tone, so Kenzie took the hint and left.

Saana shook Miriam Durham's hand and then, hooking the wheeled stool with her foot, pulled it close and sat on it.

"So, what can I do for you today?"

"Oh, it's my knees, Doctor. They're acting up something terrible. After my shifts at work, I can hardly walk, and the pain keeps me up at night too."

"Is it just your knees?" she asked as she scanned Kenzie's notes quickly.

"Oh, no, honey. It's everything—my back, too, and shooting pains down my legs—but the knees are the worst."

"Okay," she said, putting down the clipboard

and meeting Miriam's gaze. "If you have the time, I'd like to do a full examination and send you down to our lab to have some blood drawn for testing. I see here that you haven't had a full physical in five years?"

As Saana spoke to Miriam Durham, she was drawn back to the tail-end of the conversation she'd overheard between Kenzie and her patient. For some reason, hearing Miriam speak so sadly about her grandchildren lingered in her mind.

After getting some more details and the older lady's consent for the full physical, Saana got up and said, "If you'll undress down to your underwear, put on this gown and get up on the table, I'll be back in a little while."

Miriam blinked at her with an expression of rueful concern. "I'll try, but it'll take me a while. I'm not moving as fast as I used to."

Pausing on her way out the door, Saana asked, "Do you need some help? I can send the nurse back in."

"Yes, darlin'," came the reply. "Or we'll be here all night."

Smiling to herself over the patient's spicy wit, Saana exited the room in time to see Kenzie coming out of exam room four.

"Finished with Ms. Durham already?" she asked, the words carefully casual.

"No. I want to do a full examination while she's here, so I left her to put on a gown. She was asking if you could assist her in getting undressed and back up onto the table."

"Sure." Kenzie held out the chart in her hand, continuing, "Your next patient should be ready for you in a moment."

"Thanks." Taking the chart, she scanned it, again noticing the scope of Kenzie's notes. She wasn't content to just jot down the patient's blood pressure, oxygen saturation and pulse rate, but, in this case, also had *habitual smoker, diagnosed COPD three years ago*, and *not on medication initially prescribed*. All this, despite the fact the woman had come in with a stomach complaint.

Before she could say anything complimentary about the extra notations, Kenzie had already slipped past, and she heard the door shut behind her.

Suppressing a sigh at the thought of the fight they'd probably have later now that her involvement in the clinic had been revealed, Saana made her way to room four and her next patient.

It was going to be a longer night than usual, but she had only herself to blame.

She'd known how Kenzie would react but, at the time, hadn't cared. In fact, she'd been glad, thinking of it as another way to tweak at her wife's independent spirit. Now? Well, the joke was on Saana since it was coming home to her in a most unsettling way what it would mean for them to work alongside each other.

But she actually found Kenzie to be an almost ideal assistant during the shift. Of course, there were a few times her wife didn't know where to find something or a correct procedure, but the main thing in Saana's view was the way she communicated with the patients.

They all seemed perfectly at ease with her, and there were no complaints from either them or the other staff members.

Saana took a break at about seven o'clock, sitting down to finish writing up some notes and resting her feet in her office. When a knock came on her door, she sighed before calling, "Come in."

Somehow, she wasn't surprised it was Kenzie who marched in, shutting the door behind herself with a snap.

"Saana, I'm handin' in my resignation to HR tomorrow."

Leaning back in her chair, Saana gave a shrug that belied the way her heart rate kicked up, then replied, "That's up to you, but may I ask why?"

"When I said I wanted a job, I didn't mean for you to manufacture one for me. It's nepotism."

Battling annoyance, Saana kept her expression neutral, her voice cool. "What makes you think I manufactured this job for you? You wanted a job. The clinic needed a temporary nurse. I recommended they interview you, and you were hired without, may I add, any coercion from me. I put off telling HR that you're my wife for just that reason. I'll tell them tomorrow, but you got this position all on your own."

"It doesn't feel right." Kenzie's eyes were narrowed, and her lips firmed into a line.

"What about any of this feels right, Kenzie?" Suddenly exhausted, Saana rubbed a hand over her eyes, closing the lids tight for a second before meeting her wife's gaze again. "You wanted a job, and I found one for you. If you're unhappy about having to work with me, that's just too bad. Get over it."

When Kenzie looked set to start fussing again, Saana held up a hand.

"Listen, while I remember, Dr. Ramcharam has agreed to take you on as a patient. She's asking that you have your file transferred to her by your previous obstetrician, and her office called to make an appointment for this Friday morning at eleven."

"Oh." Kenzie looked startled by the change of subject and pulled out her phone. "Will you send me the address? And I'll need the information— an email, I guess—for where to send the file."

"I'll send you the phone number and email address. As for where her office is, I'll take you to the appointment myself."

"You don't have—"

Saana shook her head.

"You want us to pretend to be a couple? That

means I go to all your prenatal appointments and classes. Otherwise, what's the use of this charade?"

Even she heard the bitterness in her own voice, and so wasn't surprised when Kenzie shook her head and turned away, toward the door.

And left without another word.

CHAPTER EIGHT

SOMEHOW, THAT FIRST night of working with Saana became a turning point for Kenzie, bringing to light long-hidden truths she knew she'd have to face.

She'd harbored some misconceptions about her wife once she found out about her wealth.

In the beginning of their marriage, Kenzie had felt the relationship would work out, without doubt, once they were living in the same place. Everything had seemed wonderful, the future stretching shiny and new before them, while she was wrapping up her life in Texas in preparation for the move. Their daily telephone and video conversations had been sweet—loving. Learning about each other, sharing secrets and hopes. Looking back, she realized hints of their ultimate incompatibility had been blatant, but she'd refused to see them.

She'd already been a little intimidated by the fact Saana was a doctor who was on the verge of opening her own practice, while Kenzie had still been working on her nursing degree.

"You're only four years older than me," she'd pointed out.

Saana had shrugged it off.

"I was lucky enough to have parents who helped me get through med school," she'd replied. "It doesn't matter. At least while you're here, you can just concentrate on finishing your degree rather than working as well."

Saana had sounded so sure, so determined, that Kenzie hadn't disagreed. After all, at that time she'd had enough money saved up for the final two semesters of college and didn't have to depend on Saana to provide that for her. But all her adult life, since she'd gotten her first part-time job at fourteen, Kenzie had been used to providing for herself. Even at that young age, she'd given Aunt Lena money toward the household expenses and bought her own clothes and necessities.

She wasn't used to depending on anyone else to do for her, and she had been uneasy about the thought she might have to ask Saana for anything.

Yet she'd put that worry aside, reassuring herself it would all work out.

That had been her mantra during those weeks of wrapping up her life in San Antonio.

It will all work out.

But she hadn't known—couldn't have imagined—what she so eagerly drove toward back then.

That Saana was rich and lived a life Kenzie couldn't have even visualized. So foreign it would seem like science fiction in her wildest dreams.

And for the first time in her life, she'd severely doubted her ability to do what she'd put her mind to.

Building a life with Saana.

Making her happy.

Looking back, Kenzie knew everything she'd done, and everything Saana had done, had been seen through the framework of Saana being rich. With that much money, how could she not be out of touch with reality? And how could Kenzie ever hope to find a space for herself in that fantasy?

Seeing Saana at work—especially finding out she'd set up the clinic and trust that ran it—gave Kenzie new appreciation for her character.

The way the clinic had been set up showed a firm grasp on what the women it served really needed. So often with endeavors like this, the actual end users weren't really taken into consideration, but at the Preston Clinic it was obvious the patients were really listened to and catered to also.

And that was because Saana had the foresight

to find out their needs and make sure they would be met.

It wasn't an urgent care clinic but a place where disadvantaged women could receive the full spectrum of medical intervention—from preventative to diagnostic and specialized care, if necessary.

She was calm and listened to each patient so as to make sure they received the best treatment possible. It was truly an extension of Saana's logical and yet compassionate nature—the very nature Kenzie had been depending on when she made her desperate flight from Texas to Florida.

Deep inside, she'd known Saana wouldn't let her down. That she could depend on her wife to agree to help, even if it was to come up with another plan. One that had a better chance of working.

Everything she'd asked of her, Saana had done.

And how had Kenzie reacted in return?

Like a bit of a brat, really.

So busy thinking of herself and the babies—even though she'd been the instigator of the entire situation—that she'd spared little thought for the upheaval in Saana's life.

Yes, it was the most stressful situation Kenzie had ever been in, but the fact was that she'd caused it herself.

It was time to stop acting the fool and start being grateful for the help she was getting.

Besides, now that she knew Saana was working over twelve hours, four days a week, she was also worried. She'd always pushed herself hard, but working at both clinics was, in Kenzie's opinion, too much.

Not that she had any right to say anything about it. After all, nothing had changed from the past she'd run away from, and this situation was still temporary. Kenzie wasn't enough of an idiot to think otherwise, no matter what personal revelations she might have or her continued love for Saana. But what she could do was stop making things more difficult and even try to make Saana's life easier in whatever small ways she could.

It was hard sometimes to figure out what that might be since the distance between them lay cool and wide…

Except at night…

They'd gotten into a routine of sorts. Kenzie would say she wanted to watch the news and that Saana should have her shower first. Then Saana would come down in her robe to tell Kenzie she was finished and stay downstairs until she thought Kenzie was already in bed before going back up.

But even with that careful maneuvering, and although they started out on opposite sides of the bed, somehow Kenzie always awoke with Saana snuggled against her back—snuggled in so tight she imagined she could feel every delicious curve—and they breathed together as though they were one.

It was sweet torment to have one long arm and one leg thrown over her body, cocooning her in fragrant warmth. Reminding her of the nights when they'd made love until they were satiated, then lain that way, talking until they'd both fallen asleep.

Each night, she lay as still as possible, not wanting to move in case Saana woke up and rolled away. Torturing herself until her heart seemed fit to beat its way out of her chest and her body began to shiver with suppressed need. Only then did she move, knowing that if they stayed that way any longer, she'd roll over into Saana's arms, either courting rejection or the type of explosive encounter that could only lead to more chaos.

Now, as she put together breakfast, just thinking about those nightly encounters made a hard tremor fire down her spine.

The sound of footsteps alerted her to Saana's approach, and Kenzie took a long, deep breath in preparation.

"Hungry?" she asked when she knew her wife was within earshot. "I'm cookin' oatmeal."

"You don't have to cook breakfast for me every morning," Saana replied as she went for the coffeepot. "I usually grab something on my way to work."

Kenzie snorted. "I have to eat soon after getting up, or the babies make me feel miserable. It's no big deal to cook something for you too."

"Well, then, thank you." Pouring herself a cup, she asked, "What are your symptoms?"

"Huh?"

"When you don't eat on time. What happens?"

"Oh, a bit of nausea," she replied. "At the beginning, I was worried I'd develop hyperemesis gravidarum, the morning sickness was so bad, but it got better over time. Although, if I don't pay attention, it'll nudge me. Or the babies will."

"You're probably soon going to have to limit how much food you eat at any one time," Saana said as she moved to sit at the table. "We can come up with a diet plan to make sure you get all the nutrition you need without getting indigestion. You could mention the continued nausea to the doctor when you see her later."

"I will, although my previous obstetrician said not to worry unless it becomes unmanageable, and when I eat on time, it's fine."

After dishing out two bowls of oatmeal, Kenzie carried them to the table, where she'd already put out honey, almond milk and some mixed berries she'd found in the fridge. Sliding Saana's bowl over to her, she sat down on the opposite side of the table.

Neither of them spoke for a while as they ate, but Saana seemed to be taking her time over breakfast, and Kenzie found herself checking the clock repeatedly. Finally, unable to stop herself, she said, "Hey, if you don't get a move on, you'll be late for work."

Saana didn't look up from where she was adding a few more berries to her bowl.

"I'm not going in this morning. I got reception to reschedule my patients since I'm taking you to your appointment."

"Oh." Kenzie turned that over in her mind and then added, "Okay."

Saana's lips tightened for an instant. "I told you I was going with you. Didn't you believe me?"

"Sure did. But I just thought you'd go to work as usual and we'd meet there. This is good, though. Better."

"Why better?" Saana asked, tone still cool but seemingly unable to resist her curiosity.

"Well, you work twelve-hour days for most of the week. A little time to yourself probably isn't a bad thing."

Saana's gaze lifted then, and Kenzie found herself suddenly breathless. Then Saana glanced down again.

"It is tiring," she admitted, her voice low, making it seem like saying the words out loud was somehow taboo. "But the clinic is still so new. I have to be on top of things."

Kenzie snorted before she could stop herself.

How like Saana to have to be in control all the time, even when it might not be completely necessary.

"It's true," Saana interjected before Kenzie could reply. "Right now, there aren't enough doctors on staff for me not to be there."

"Can't the trust hire some more staff?"

Saana pushed her bowl away and leaned back, crossing her arms.

"Hopefully, they will be able to soon, but for the time being, we have the make do with the doctors we have."

It brought to mind a question Kenzie had been pondering since learning about the clinic, and she didn't see the harm in asking.

"How did the whole clinic idea come about, anyway?"

Saana relaxed, her arms falling away from their defensive posture.

"I worked in a free clinic when I was in med school, initially just for the experience, but then I saw just how necessary places like those can be. Yet the entire time I was there, I kept thinking how I would improve on the services, widen the scope, if it were mine. I shelved the idea for a while so I could build up my practice, but it was always in the back of my mind."

It wasn't hard to see Saana having an idea and just going for it. Focus was another of her character traits. "Okay, but that doesn't explain the name. How did you come up with that?"

There was a part of her—the part that had jealously come up with the idea that Saana had found someone else—that expected not to get a reply. Somewhere, deep inside, Kenzie thought she knew the answer: that the clinic and trust had been named for whoever it was her wife was now in love with, even though Saana had claimed there wasn't anyone else.

"That was easy." A ghost of a smile tipped the corners of Saana's lips. "It's Mom's maiden name, and I got the money I used to set up the trust from my grandfather George. His will stipulated that I couldn't touch the principle until I turned thirty-five, so I had to wait."

She'd turned thirty-five the year before, and a sudden rush of sadness for not having been there to celebrate the milestone pushed aside Kenzie's elation at knowing the origins of the Preston name.

Obviously, being around this woman was turning her into a mess, emotionally.

As usual.

Needing to lighten her own mood, she forced a grin and joked, "Grandpa didn't trust you not to spend all that cash on wine, women and song, huh?"

For the first time since Kenzie had been back in Florida, she saw Saana throw back her head and laugh. Not a chuckle or a restrained smile but a full-on riot of laughter. Seeing it brought a rush of love and want so strong it took everything Kenzie had not to round the table and absorb that humor through her kisses.

Saana was still chuckling as she replied, "Could be. Truthfully, though, I think it was just one of those things they usually do when there's that much money involved, to avoid taxes or something. He set it up the same way for Robbie, too, so at least I know it wasn't because I'm female. And I was allowed to withdraw some of the interest each year if I wanted or needed it. That helped with the maintenance of the house, but I really wanted as much as I could for the clinic, so I didn't dip into it very often."

She didn't want to talk about the house, so Kenzie kept the conversation on the clinic.

"So, you set up the trust, but it isn't enough to hire more doctors?"

Saana leaned forward, her face alight with enthusiasm.

"It cost a bomb to buy all the equipment I wanted for the clinic, and the financial advisors were honest about how long the clinic would be able to operate if the trust wasn't increased. I don't want the clinic to only last for twenty or thirty years. I want it to exist for as long as it's needed. Which reminds me: we're having a fundraising gala at Mom and Dad's house next month, and I'd like you to go with me."

Startled, Kenzie asked, "Me? Why?"

Saana raised her eyebrows. "I thought it would be obvious. You're my wife. Being there will show your support, both for me and for the clinic itself—especially since you're now working there."

"I don't think my bein' there will be a benefit to either you or the clinic," Kenzie said slowly, while her heart went a million miles an hour, and an anxious flush overwhelmed her body. "I'm sure it'll be real fancy, and we both know I'm anything but. I wouldn't even know what to wear, or…or…" She wracked her brain for the worst thing she could think of. "Or what fork to use at dinner."

Saana just shook her head, and the look on her face made Kenzie's heart rate go up a notch but not out of fear.

"I've never asked you to be anything but yourself," she said quietly while Kenzie drowned a little in those gleaming eyes. Then Saana's expression smoothed out, becoming cool again, and she gave one of those *I don't really care* shrugs. "And I know a place in Orlando where we can get you something appropriate to wear. It would look strange if you, as my wife, aren't in attendance, and it's that type of situation we need to avoid, isn't it?"

Recognizing the trap but unable to avoid it, Kenzie swallowed and then nodded.

"Yeah, I guess it is," she acknowledged since her brain couldn't come up with a good reason to get out of going. "Nobody else would care, I don't think—but your parents would think it weird, anyway."

"Exactly."

Pushing back her chair, Saana got up and stretched, making Kenzie's mouth water at the sight. There was something about that long, sleek body, those firm breasts rising on a deep inhalation that created inescapable hunger deep in Kenzie's heart and soul.

And especially in her body.

Then one of the babies kicked, as if to remind her of its presence, and, ridiculously flustered, Kenzie got up too.

"What time do we have to leave to get to Dr. Ramcharam's office?" she asked as she gathered up the dishes.

"Ten fifteen at the latest. I'm sure although they got your records, there'll be forms to fill out before your appointment."

"Yeah. Okay." She was at the sink now, her back to Saana, so she was able to draw in a deep, slightly tremulous breath without it being obvious. "I'll be ready by then."

"Why don't you leave the dishes for Delores?" Saana asked. "Come join me by the pool for a little while. I'm going to enjoy being outside for a change."

For a minute, Kenzie hesitated, tempted beyond all reason.

For the first time since she'd come back, they were talking the way they used to—openly, without the barriers that had built up while they'd been apart. Kenzie had been determined to keep her feelings in check, and if you didn't count during those embraces at night, she'd succeeded pretty well.

But just now, she was raw, each nerve a receptor, not of physical sensation but of emotion, and she knew if she wasn't careful, she'd lose her head.

Again.

As she reached for the sponge, she found her voice and replied, "You go ahead. Maybe I'll come out when I'm finished."

That was a lie, though.

She needed time to pull herself together and rebuild those defenses against the love and need washing through her system.

She held her breath until she heard Saana's footsteps retreat into the distance, and then she let it out with a whoosh.

She'd be spending most of the rest of the day with her wife. Best take some time to regroup and get herself under control.

As if agreeing, one of the babies—or was it both?—did something that felt like a karate kick.

"Yes," she muttered. "Just think of the babies, and you'll be okay."

Only the babies.

Nothing else.

CHAPTER NINE

KENZIE SEEMED PARTICULARLY quiet on the drive over to the obstetrician's office, and Saana made no effort to fill the silence. Although they'd always been able to sit together without talking, to her the air in the car felt heavy, heralding that some undefinable change had taken place between them.

Finally, unable to resist breaking the tension, Saana asked, "Nervous about your appointment?"

A glance caught Kenzie giving an ironic little smile.

"Nah. I feel good, and I know the babies are growin' like crazy. My belly's gotten so big I'm guessing I'll have to start using a rideshare service to get to work soon. The steering wheel's getting closer and closer."

"Well, you do have a workmate who can drive you in each afternoon."

She said it lightly, trying to get back that easy camaraderie they'd seemed to achieve this morning over breakfast but had lost again somehow.

"That doesn't make sense, considerin' where your other office is in comparison to the house and the clinic. It shouldn't cost too much, so don't worry about it."

Classic Kenzie, unwilling—almost unable—to accept even the slightest bit of help.

Except when it came to the lives in her uterus.

So, although she wanted to argue, Saana let it drop.

At Dr. Ramcharam's office, Kenzie filled out the requisite forms, and thankfully it wasn't long before they were called back to the exam room. When Saana got up with her, Kenzie seemed to hesitate for an instant before following the nurse, and although Saana felt a spurt of annoyance, she again kept quiet.

After the weigh-in and the other usual tests and questions, the nurse handed Kenzie a gown and said, "Strip down—although you can keep your bra on, if you want—and put this on, please. Dr. Ramcharam will be with you in a few minutes."

It was then Saana recognized the position she'd put herself in and frantically wondered how to get out of it.

"Do you want me to…"

Already having pulled her blouse off over her head, Kenzie glanced over and cocked an eyebrow.

"What?"

"Um… I was wondering if you wanted me to leave while you got undressed?"

By then, the baggy shorts Kenzie had been wearing were already in a puddle around her ankles, in preparation of her stepping out of them.

"Nah. There's nothing you haven't seen already," she said, but Saana thought her voice sounded strange. A little deeper than usual. "Besides, you know I ain't shy."

Her drawl was more pronounced, but Saana hardly noticed, her gaze intent on Kenzie's body, so enthrallingly changed and yet so gloriously familiar.

Pregnancy suited Kenzie, in every way. Saana had always loved her wife's bountiful curves, but somehow now she looked even more enticing. It wasn't something Saana had ever considered before, but who knew pregnant women could be so terribly arousing?

In what seemed like slow motion, Kenzie pushed down her tiny tap pants and, once they were off, stooped to pick them and her shorts up.

It was like watching a gorgeous statue come to life. Strong thigh muscles, round bottom, full breasts and the prominent bulge of her belly were emphasized in the movement. It was a moment she had no doubt she'd remember for the rest of the life. Kenzie arose, her body once more showcased in profile, and heat flashed from Saana's chest into her face, her mouth going dry as her heart thumped like a mad thing in her chest.

Standing with hands on hips, Kenzie met Saana's gaze.

"Why're you lookin' at me like that?"

No mistaking the gravel in those drawled words, but it took a moment to actually comprehend what Kenzie had asked.

"You're so damn beautiful…"

Kenzie's eyelids drooped, but then she shook her head and turned away to grab the smock.

As she thrust her arms into the sleeves, she said, "Thanks, but wrong time and definitely wrong place."

Will there ever be a right time and place again?

But even as she opened her mouth to ask the silly, hopeful question, there was a knock on the door, and Maria Ramcharam came in.

"McKenzie? I'm Dr. Ramcharam," she said, coming in with her hand outstretched. Then she noticed Saana, and her dark gaze tracked from one woman to the other as she shook Kenzie's hand. "Nice to see you, Saana."

It came out more like a question than a statement, and Saana couldn't help smiling slightly.

"Kenzie is my wife, Maria."

The slightly curious expression on the doctor's face was wiped away, leaving it expressionless.

"Oh. Lovely. Hop up here, McKenzie, and let's take a look at you."

Kenzie chuckled. "No hoppin' goin' on here right now. Not with this belly in front of me."

As Kenzie went to step up on the footstep, Saana held out her hand to offer support and was pleased when Kenzie immediately took it.

"I had a look at your records," Maria said, glancing at the laptop where her nurse had entered Kenzie's results for weight, blood pressure, glucose levels and O-sat. "And I'm quite happy with your progress. Of course, I'm sure you know that going forward, your twins will be gaining weight rapidly."

As she asked questions and listened intently to Kenzie's responses, Maria measured Kenzie's belly and then palpated it.

"One head here," she said before running her hand along Kenzie's left side. "Bottom here. And… Here we go. There's the other head. I'm going to do an ultrasound, just to see how things are shaping up inside. It's important, with twins especially, to keep a check on the amniotic fluid."

"It'll be nice if the second baby decides to let me know their sex," Kenzie said with another chuckle.

"I noticed one was hiding the information in the last ultrasound," Maria said, smiling as she prepared the machine. "Let's see if we can encourage him or her to solve the mystery."

Kenzie hissed as the gel was applied, drawing Saana's gaze from the monitor to her face. She was obviously eager, and her delight—apparent in the sweet curve of lips and twinkling eyes—made Saana's heart melt.

"Here's your little man," Maria said. "And…"

She paused, and Saana saw Kenzie's eyes widen.

"A girl!" It was Kenzie who said it, and sudden radiance made her expression joyous. "It is a girl, isn't it?"

"Yes."

And Saana was unbearably moved when Kenzie, still looking at the monitor, reached blindly for her hand and said, "Oh, Saana. One of each. Isn't that awesome?"

"Beautiful," Saana replied, although all she could see was Kenzie's smile. "Absolutely beautiful."

The clinic was busy that Friday evening, but Kenzie was still buzzing with happiness and didn't mind being kept hopping.

One of each!

When she'd first been told that two of the four implanted eggs had taken, she'd immediately hoped for a girl and a boy. Back then, she was glad for Darryl and Ashley's sake. Now, she was ecstatic for her own.

It just felt *right*.

All of it.

None of her fears and apprehension could touch the happiness rushing through her blood. Not about how quiet Saana had been on the drive back from Dr. Ramcharam's office, nor what was going to happen with the custody. Not even what leaving Saana again would do to her heart.

None of it could touch her tonight.

As she walked swiftly down the corridor to call the next patient in, Kenzie was humming a country song under her breath.

"You're in a chipper mood tonight," Minerva said as they met up at the main desk.

"Feelin' like a million bucks," Kenzie replied with a grin. "Babies doin' well, and the little girl finally decided to let us in on the secret of her sex. It's a good day."

Minerva grinned back and nodded once. "Sounds like it."

That was all the time they had to chat, though. The waiting room was full, but thankfully, there were four doctors in the clinic that night, so they should be able to get to everyone.

Most of the patients were referrals and had appointments, but there were also a few walk-ins—women who'd heard about the clinic and came there in hopes of being seen. While they could always go to the emergency room of any of the local hospitals, word had gotten around that the clinic was an easier alternative if you were in that area. What Kenzie realized was that the women were coming in with their complaints earlier than they might have gone to the hospital. Coming in while their ills were still fairly easily treated rather than trying to stick it out until they were too sick to go on.

If that was the only reason the clinic existed, it would be a really good one, in Kenzie's opinion. Some of the patients she'd seen in the ER back in San Antonio, who knew they couldn't afford a doctor or medicine, had waited until it was too late.

As she went to the door separating the waiting room from the nurses' station, she heard someone shout, "Can we get some help here?"

Pushing the handle to open the door, Kenzie rushed to the aid of an older woman, who was supporting a younger, taller and heavier one around the waist, obviously straining under the weight.

"What happened?" she asked, putting her arm around the sagging woman from the other side, bracing to help hold her up.

"I don't know," the woman on the other side replied. "She just came through the door, stopped, then looked like she was going to fall over."

Minerva, seeing what was happening, came running with a wheelchair, and between herself and Kenzie, they were able to ease the young woman into it. When they settled her in the chair, her head lolled back so Kenzie was looking into unfocused eyes.

"Get the door," Minerva said, and Kenzie ran ahead to do just that. Then, as the chair rolled through, she hurried to catch up and reached for the woman's wrist, feeling the rapid pulse.

"Get one of the doctors," Minerva snapped to the receptionist as they rushed past the front desk. "And you better call an ambulance too."

Kenzie pushed open the door to exam room one, which she knew was empty, and Minerva maneuvered the wheelchair through. Between them, they were able to get the patient onto the examination table, and both nurses started preliminary tests, calling out to each other so as not to double up and waste time.

By the time they'd taken BP, O-sat and pulse rate, the door burst open, and Saana came barreling in.

"What do we have?" she asked before she even got to the table.

"She collapsed just as she came in through the door," Minerva replied before reading out the levels they'd already collected.

"BP is high. Glucose?" Saana asked as she lifted first one, then the other of the patient's eyelids to check her pupils.

"Normal," Kenzie said, having just got the reading.

"Minerva, please check to see if anyone came in with her, and call an ambulance."

"Ambulance should be on the way," Minerva said as she headed for the door. "I'll see if anyone knows her."

"Hey," Saana said, tapping the patient's cheek gently. "Hey, can you hear me?"

The patient muttered; then one eye opened.

"Hi, there." Saana leaned closer, making sure she was in the other woman's line of sight. "Can you tell me your name?"

Her mouth opened, but what came out was a garbled mishmash of sound, and her fear was unmistakable. Her right hand came up, grasping at Saana, who took it in her own hand.

"You're okay." She made her voice soothing. "I'm Dr. Ameri, and we're looking after you."

The patient, instead of calming down, grew more frantic, babbling and moving restlessly on the table. Kenzie moved up close to Saana.

"I'll keep trying to calm her down so you can go on with the examination."

They switched places, and as Saana turned toward the cupboard where the instruments were, Kenzie saw the patient's hand lower so that it rested on her belly. The familiarity of the gesture—fingers cupped below the navel, thumb above—made her heart jolt.

"Saana," she said quietly, forgetting professionalism in the urgency of the moment. "I think she might be pregnant. That's what she's been trying to tell us."

As the wail of the approaching ambulance ratcheted Kenzie's tension higher, Saana turned to meet her gaze, and for an instant the same fear she felt was reflected back at her. Then her wife spun away to reach into the cupboard and grab a fetal Doppler.

Minerva came back in just then.

"Someone in the waiting room thinks they know where this woman lives. She's run to the house, to see if anyone's there."

Minerva paused, seeing Saana with the fetal heart monitor, and her lips tightened for a swift second. Kenzie could see the flashes of red lights coming around the edges of the blinds and tried to pull herself together. She felt disembodied. Mentally and emotionally adrift, as recognition of what was happening to the young patient forced itself onto her consciousness.

Saana didn't have to say anything. Neither did Minerva. Kenzie saw all the signs of some type of cerebrovascular incident—whether it was a stroke or aneurysm wouldn't be known until she got to the hospital—but a pregnancy would make the emergency all the more urgent.

Then came the *whoosh-whoosh-whoosh* of a tiny heartbeat, and Kenzie's stomach clenched.

"McKenzie." Minerva's voice startled her back

to the moment. "Go and lead the paramedics in. Make sure they hurry."

She didn't reply. Her throat had closed with the type of emotion she normally didn't allow herself at work. Rushing out of the exam room, she hoped to collect herself before anyone noticed how shaken she was. Cutting through a short passageway leading to the nearest emergency exit, she used her cloth-covered shoulder to wipe her eyes before pushing the door open.

The paramedics were pulling the gurney out of the back of the vehicle when she called, "This way."

But when they got to the exam room, she didn't go in with them but instead slipped away to the bathroom, where she stripped off her gloves, then washed her hands and face. The face that looked back at her from the mirror looked older than the one she'd seen in the morning—but she shrugged the thought away.

"Pregnancy hormones," she said to herself as she dried her hands. "That's all."

With one last deep breath, she tossed the paper towels into the bin and went back to work, determined to regain, and maintain, her workday persona.

She thought she'd done okay until later that night, when her restless sleep was interrupted once more by the sensation of Saana snuggled against her back. Where before it had been arousing, tonight she felt tears threaten once more because it felt like home.

Like safety.

As if no matter what, the woman whose arm was wrapped around her wouldn't allow anything bad to happen.

It was frightening. She'd always known she could take care of herself. At least, that's what she'd told herself and anyone else who would listen.

But tonight, she didn't have the strength. So, when Saana finally stirred, seemingly about to roll away, Kenzie gripped her wrist and held on.

Saana didn't hesitate, but placed her hand back over Kenzie's belly and went back to sleep. And Kenzie, feeling the stress leech away, followed suit.

CHAPTER TEN

SATURDAY MORNING DAWNED overcast and gray, strangely echoing Saana's mood. The emotion she'd felt the night before, even before Kenzie's fingers closed on her wrist, had kept her awake for hours and even now lingered.

Her mind, usually so ordered and meticulous, couldn't seem to stop spinning—swinging wildly from one thought to the next.

It had been easy to see the effect their emergency patient had on Kenzie. Just the expression on her face, the fear in her eyes, had sent a shock of apprehension through Saana's body too. For the rest of the evening, although Kenzie had been her usual capable self, there'd been an atmosphere of disconnect between what she was doing or saying and the flatness of her affect. Her words didn't match her expression. Smiles didn't seem natural or reach her eyes. The empathy she usually displayed had still been there but from a distance.

That anxiety was as contagious as the flu and

had awakened all Saana's protective instincts. But just because Kenzie had been obviously shaken by their patient's situation didn't mean anything had changed. Kenzie wouldn't be grateful if Saana started coddling her, the way she wanted to. In fact, it would probably cause more tension, increasing the problem.

It would be so much easier if she just didn't give a damn. If she could maintain some kind of detachment from Kenzie. Yet she was forced to acknowledge that each and every day they were together made Kenzie even more fascinating than she'd been before.

Made Saana fall even further in love.

Sighing, she swung her feet off the bed, wondering how best to handle the increasingly complex mess they'd created together. None of her experience in life had prepared her for this conundrum.

In the past, she would have simply taken control. Or tried to. She'd have marched downstairs and told Kenzie to stop working, for the sake of her emotional well-being and the well-being of the babies.

She couldn't stop the little snort of unamused laughter that broke from her throat at that thought. It would never have worked. Kenzie valued her independence far too much to give in to such a suggestion. In fact, she'd have fought it tooth and nail in her quiet, implacable way.

And who could blame her, really?

Kenzie had been working since she was a teenager. Longer, if you count being her aunt Lena's right hand since she was even younger. Unless the doctor put her on bed rest, she'd keep working until the twins were born. She'd be climbing the walls with boredom and fretting about her future finances if she stayed home with nothing to do.

But...

It didn't mean Saana was totally without resources when it came to protecting Kenzie. She just had to be strategic about it and keep her own emotions out of the equation.

In reality, that would be the hardest part.

Determined but still apprehensive, she went downstairs, expecting to find Kenzie in the kitchen or the small den she favored when at home, but she wasn't in either place. Moving into the great room at the back of the house, Saana looked out toward the river and saw Kenzie sitting by the dock.

Funny to think it had been only a week since the last time she'd walked down the garden path to speak to her wife about her request for help. It felt as though those intervening years when they'd been apart had faded way. Become insignificant.

Dangerous territory, in line with the Santayana quote about those who forget the past...

Not something she could afford. So she forced her emotions down deep, pulling her cloak of cool control around herself. Hiding beneath it.

Kenzie looked over her shoulder at Saana's approach, and the dark shadows beneath her eyes were obvious.

"Mornin'," she said with a small smile.

"Good morning." Saana sank onto the bench next to her, making no attempt to hide the way she was scrutinizing her wife. "You didn't sleep well last night, did you?"

Kenzie looked away, over the water.

"Got some sleep. I'm okay."

"Really?" Letting her skepticism show, she shook her head. "Could have fooled me."

The sound Kenzie made was neither amused nor annoyed but seemed to fall somewhere in between.

"Why not just say I look like hell on wheels and be done?"

A shrug seemed the appropriate response, and it was easy to keep her tone cool when those dark eyes weren't focused on her. "Because you never look like hell on wheels, but you do look tired. I have to run out to get something. Why don't you come with me, and we can go to Ernest's Tavern, where they have those delicious egg Bennies, for breakfast?"

"I can make breakfast here."

"I know you can."

No use pushing. Better to let Kenzie make the decision herself.

"I wonder if they ever found out that young girl's name."

She didn't have to specify. Saana had suspected it might be weighing on her mind, which was why she'd called the hospital before heading down to the dock.

"Yes, they did. They were able to treat her quickly enough and think she'll make a full recovery. She was able to tell them her name and where to contact her boyfriend."

"And the baby?"

"Doing well." It had been on the tip of her tongue to add *so far*, but she bit the words back. Not so much because she thought she'd be shielding Kenzie, who would no doubt know the continued risk, but so as to keep the news upbeat. Hopefully, that would lift Kenzie's spirits.

Kenzie let out a breath as if she'd been holding the air in her lungs while waiting for the reply. Then, with a little shake of her shoulders, she rose.

"Yeah. Let's go get some breakfast. Then maybe I'll take a nap before work this afternoon."

Relieved, Saana got up too.

"It'll just take me a minute to get ready," Kenzie said as they headed back to the house.

"Take your time. There's no rush. I'm going to grab a coffee."

As Saana went into the kitchen, she was genuinely surprised both by Kenzie's actions and the relief she felt at them. She'd been wondering how to get Kenzie to relax, maybe even sleep a little before work, but hadn't had to do much except invite her to breakfast.

Apparently, cool and controlled was the way to go when trying to manage her wife. It went against everything Saana wanted to do, but if that was what it took, she'd have to keep it up.

As glad as she was that the young woman patient had been successfully treated and that her baby was fine, Kenzie couldn't shake the sense of gloom that had been dogging her since the night before.

As she started getting the examination rooms prepared for the evening clinic, her brain kept cycling back to the fear in the other woman's eyes.

The desperation.

And, like the refrain of a song when the record kept skipping back, she heard Aunt Lena's voice in her head: *You never know the luck of a mangy mutt.*

Most people used it in a positive way, meaning that just because you were down and out didn't mean something good couldn't happen.

But Aunt Lena used it both as an expression of hope and of warning.

Just because you were down and out didn't mean something worse might not happen.

Luck was capricious.

Life was capricious.

Not that Kenzie didn't already know that. She'd been through enough in her lifetime to realize how little control she had over the really important issues. But it wasn't something that had affected her emotionally. Not the way the thought of something happening to her and the babies was scrambling her brain.

To the point of being so scared she felt completely and utterly powerless.

The early part of the day had passed in a blur. At breakfast, Saana had kept the conversation going, chatting about inconsequential things while Kenzie picked at her meal and tried to respond appropriately. She'd like to think it was tiredness from a disturbed night of sleep making her feel like she was underwater, but it was much more than that.

Not even a nap before work had made it go away.

The door to the examination room swung open, and Minerva came in.

"Everything okay in here?"

"Sure," Kenzie replied, trying to sound like

she meant it. "I've restocked both rooms, and we're ready to rock and roll."

"Good." The head nurse took a quick look around, as she did each evening before the clinic opened. "Hopefully, tonight won't be as eventful as last night was."

Kenzie was glad to have her back to the other woman so she wouldn't see her wince.

"Yeah," she finally said, when she was sure her voice would be normal.

As Kenzie turned to head out the door, Minerva hitched her hip on the wall and said, "By the way, I realized you and Dr. Saana knew each other from before but didn't realize you were such good friends."

"What do you mean?"

Taken by surprise, that was all she could think of to ask.

"Well, I saw you getting out of her car this afternoon."

It hadn't even occurred to her that their traveling to the clinic together would cause any kind of stir, and now she was left floundering to think of what to say.

How much easier it would be to simply admit they were married, but they hadn't discussed the matter, and Kenzie was reluctant to be the one to out them.

So instead, she pulled herself together to say,

"She was nice enough to offer me a drive since we were coming from the same direction."

Minerva's eyebrows went up.

"You live in the same neighborhood as Dr. Ameri?" Her skepticism was clear. Then her hand flew to her mouth, and her eyes widened. "Oh my God, McKenzie. I'm so sorry. That sounded horrible. I didn't mean—"

After a snort of laughter, Kenzie replied, "No worries. I'm not surprised. I'm definitely not in the same league as Saana."

"Stop that," Minerva said, sounding caught somewhere between horror and amusement. "You're a lovely person. It's just that I know the doctor's family is loaded…" She stopped and shook her head, her hands flapping as if she was trying to shut herself up. "I'm making it worse, aren't I?"

Kenzie just laughed and opened the door.

"Don't worry about it. You haven't hurt my feelings."

Saana was right outside the door, and both Kenzie and Minerva paused when they saw her standing there, her head slightly tilted, as though in question.

"'Scuse me," Kenzie muttered, sidestepping her wife while trying to avoid that interrogative look. "Time for the first patient."

Walking away, she could swear she felt Saana's gaze boring into her, but even as the skin at the back of her neck heated, she kept going without looking back.

At least the conversation with Minerva had given her something else to think about other than her fears and allowed her to better concentrate on her patients' needs as the evening wore on.

Finally, the final patient had been seen, and they cleaned up the examination rooms, doing a quick restock as needed. Saana was sitting in the cubicle off the nurses' station, writing up the last of her notes, when Minerva stopped Kenzie as she was walking toward the lockers.

"Hey, do you need a ride home?"

From the corner of her eye, Kenzie saw Saana's head come up and knew she was listening.

"No thanks, Minerva. I'm good."

"You sure? It's not a problem."

Saana stood up, and Kenzie said quickly, "I have a ride already, so thanks but no thanks."

"Okay—but you know, if you need a ride, you can always call me rather than bothering Dr. Ameri."

"Sure. Thanks," she said quickly, starting to walk away, not wanting to get any deeper into the conversation.

But a quick look back showed Saana striding in the opposite direction, and something about that prowling gait rang all kinds of alarms in Kenzie's head.

There was nothing said on the ride home, but the air between them hummed with a kind of electricity that had Kenzie wondering which one of them was giving it off. Her previous gloomy mood was submerged beneath this new jumpiness, and she would be hard-pressed to say which of those feelings was worse.

Getting to the house, Saana parked her car in the garage, and they went inside, still silent. Tired to the bone, Kenzie made a beeline for the stairs, but Saana called her name, halting her flight.

"I could see you were upset by the situation last night, so I bought a blood pressure monitor for you," she said, as cool as ever. "I'll be monitoring your BP morning and night, just to be on the safe side."

"Thanks," she mumbled, turning away so Saana couldn't see the tears welling in her eyes. Somehow the thoughtfulness coupled with that emotionless delivery was more painful than she'd expected.

"No problem." Kenzie's foot was on the first step when Saana's voice once more made her stop. "Why didn't you tell Minerva that you lived here with me?"

Surprise had Kenzie turning to face her wife. "What?"

"When Minerva was offering you a ride home, why didn't you just tell her we were married?"

"It's none of her business, for one," she replied, strangely glad for the change of subject, which took her mind completely off Saana's consideration. "And second, I didn't want to stir up any trouble at work. I'm only going to be there until your original nurse comes back, so why make it difficult?"

"Difficult?" Saana pronounced the word as if she wasn't sure what it meant. "For whom?"

Kenzie rolled her eyes. "For either of us. You want folks chatting behind our backs, sayin' whatever they feel like about our relationship?"

"I don't really care what anyone says about our relationship." Her voice had gone from cool to icy. "Why should I?"

"Wow." The spark of anger heating her stomach at Saana's arrogance was welcome. "Easy for you to say. Let's be honest here… No one's gonna give you sideways looks and whisper about *your* motives for being in the marriage. I'd be the one taking the heat, right? Bein' called a gold digger or worse."

Saana's eyes narrowed, and her lips tightened.

"Do you really think it's wise to try to pretend we aren't married?"

"I'm not pretending we're not married," Kenzie replied, her voice rising to match the racing of her heart. "I'm just not tellin' every Tom, Dick and Harry we are. What's wrong with that, especially when I'm gonna be gone again in a while? Wouldn't *you* prefer they didn't know, under those circumstances? When we both know this isn't a long-term situation?"

"What I would prefer isn't of any importance. And the long term doesn't concern me. It's the short term I'm thinking about." Saana moved closer so they were within touching distance, and Kenzie could have sworn she felt the heat coming in waves off her wife's body. "You want to make it seem our marriage is solid for the sake of your children. That means being open about it, not hiding because you're worried what people will say. It also means publicly being my wife."

Then she gave one of those dismissive shrugs that said oh so clearly how little she cared about any of it. "Besides, in three weeks, when we have our first fundraiser, I expect you to be there. Not as an employee of the clinic but as my supportive, loving wife. So no matter how difficult it might be, I suggest you start acting that way."

The jolt Kenzie felt when Saana brushed past her to head up the stairs stole her breath.

Saana raised her hand to grasp the banister, her back as straight as a board, defiance and dismissiveness blatant in every line of that slim, sexy body.

A rush of emotion—love, anger, want—made Kenzie's blood boil, but a little voice in the back of her head whispered a memory and kept her rooted in place…

She was walking alongside Saana down the strip in Las Vegas, wondering why the woman who'd been so warm and enticing earlier in the day had turned cool and somehow distant. A gust of wind rustled past, causing Saana to raise her hand to brush a wisp of hair off her face, allowing Kenzie to see how her fingers trembled.

And it was then Kenzie recognized the attraction between them had grown past just liking but that Saana wasn't sure what to do about it. How to express her needs. Instead, it was bottled up inside, vibrating through her, just like it fired in waves through Kenzie too.

There was a little recess beside where they were walking, and Kenzie impulsively reached for Saana's wrist, tugging her into the niche so they stood face-to-face, bodies brushing with each inhale.

"I want you."

Kenzie made it a statement and a question all in one, sensing Saana needed her to take the lead but wanting her to feel comfortable enough to refuse.

"Come back to my room."

"Yes."

It was barely a whisper, and Saana leaned closer so the word brushed like a feather against Kenzie's lips.

"Yes."

How had she forgotten that moment until now?

Let the knowledge slip away of how her wife dealt with desire when she wasn't sure it would be reciprocated?

Until seeing the unmistakable trembling of Saana's fingers as she reached for the banister.

Kenzie wondered how to handle the situation even as her heart galloped and arousal became a flame threatening to incinerate her from the inside out. She wanted Saana, desperately, but hadn't she decided complicating the situation by making love to her would be stupid? Did she really want to compound her heartbreak by getting that close?

But hadn't they already stepped past the rules they'd imposed on the situation? And mightn't it actually be better to deal with this overwhelming desire rather than let frustrations create arguments and discord?

Even as she thought it, Kenzie knew she was just finding excuses to do what she wanted.

Make love to Saana, no matter where doing so might lead.

So determination and erotic intent overcame common sense, and she set off after her wife.

CHAPTER ELEVEN

SAANA STRIPPED DOWN and stepped into the shower, shivering as the water hit her over-sensitized skin.

It was very probable, she thought, that she was losing her mind in increments each day Kenzie remained in the house. Lying beside her, night after night, was torture, especially since her slumbering self couldn't seem to stay on her own side of the bed, instead giving in and seeking the closeness it craved.

Saana moaned under her breath, remembering the sensations of Kenzie's body against hers, the firm satin skin under her hands. No one had ever demanded her surrender until Kenzie, and no one else had ever given her the type of ecstasy she'd experienced under her wife's concentrated, passion-inducing attention.

No one else had been able to make her lose all control. Get her so aroused she wanted to beg for orgasm and yet knew if she waited, gave in to the desire, she would experience all the release she could ever need.

Often multiple times.

And no one but Kenzie had made her inhibitions fall away until there was nothing Saana wouldn't do to give her wife the same pleasure she'd meted out.

Kenzie had introduced her to a side of herself—a wanton, rapacious side—that Saana would have hitherto absolutely denied.

The side that had died when Kenzie left but now was rampaging behind the calm facade Saana presented to the world.

With another muffled groan, she lifted her face to the water streaming from above and reached for the tap to decrease the hot water flowing through. But before she could make the change to the cold shower she so desperately needed, the bathroom door opened, freezing her in place.

Beyond the glass enclosure, crossing the bathroom, came Kenzie, gloriously naked.

The effect on Saana was immediate. Goose bumps arose all over her body, her breath got trapped in her lungs and her muscles tightened, affected by the wild spurt of adrenaline into her bloodstream induced by the fight-or-flight instinct.

Yet, as Kenzie pulled open the door and stepped into the shower, Saana neither fought nor fled.

"Wh…? Wha…?"

Kenzie reached for the body wash and scrubby, her lips tilted into a smile.

"You said I was to act like your wife, so I decided to come and wash your back. It was one of the things I always used to do, so I figured it would be a good way to get back into the role." Then she lifted one eyebrow. "Do you want me to do it or not?"

Unable to find her voice, Saana turned her back to Kenzie and stood shivering under the water.

"I thought this might help," Kenzie said as she squirted soap onto the scrubby. "We both know where our relationship is goin'—or in our case, not goin'—but it doesn't mean we're not still attracted to each other. All this sexual tension makes it hard to act naturally when we're together, don't ya think?"

Think? Kenzie wanted her to think while they were naked in the shower together, and Saana knew those hands—so skilled in the art of love—would soon be on her body?

She tried to laugh, but it came out a weird, strangled wheeze. Then Kenzie stroked the scrubby down the length of her spine, and Saana braced against the wall to hold herself up.

"Now, I can wash your back and leave," Kenzie said, her drawl getting slower. Sexier. "Or I can stay, and we can relieve a bunch of the stress that's been building up the last few days. It's completely up to you."

Saana cursed silently. How much easier it would be if Kenzie just took over without giving her a choice. But although Saana knew her wife was definitely more dominant in their sexual relationship, Kenzie had never pushed or forced.

She'd always asked for consent.

For the type of complete complicity that turned Saana on more easily than anything else.

After clearing her throat, Saana whispered, "It might make it worse, though. I'm struggling, trying not to get pulled in any deeper with you, Kenzie, but you're making it so difficult."

Kenzie froze for a moment, then gave a wry chuckle. "I know what you mean. It all went so bad the last time, but I doubt our situation could get much more complicated, no matter what we do."

"Why did it go wrong? I've never really understood."

Even raising that minefield of a question couldn't douse the heat under her skin as Kenzie shifted, her breast gliding across Saana's back.

"I'm not really sure." Kenzie's voice was low and rough, as though the admission hurt to make. "But what I do know is that I'm goin' crazy, sleeping beside you every night, trying to stop myself from touchin' you. If you're havin' the same problem, then let's do somethin' about it. We can sort the rest of it out another time, when my head is clear. Right now, all I can think about is touching you. Tasting you. Making you come so hard you can't help crying out."

If she refused, she thought she'd just go up in flames and burn away to ash with frustration; yet still, Saana hesitated, trying to find the willpower to walk away. But with each stroke of the scrubby—now working sideways, going lower to her waist, almost to her bottom—Saana fell deeper under Kenzie's spell.

She'd always been under her spell, she thought almost despairingly. No one had ever gotten under her skin, into her head and heart like Kenzie. Wishing she could explain that while for Kenzie, it might be just sex, for her it was so much more. It had been clear from the moment they met. Sexual attraction was a big part of it, for sure, but what Saana felt in her heart for her wife far surpassed that.

It was love, pure and simple, with all the care and concern, the longing and fear and desperation and anxiety that came with it. But right now, with her heart pounding and need clawing at her, she had to accept the truth.

There was no use in lying when she knew Kenzie was right. If they went on like this for much longer—aroused and unfulfilled—they'd be at each other's throats soon.

So she took a deep breath, turned to face her wife and said, "Stay."

The first time they'd kissed, Kenzie had felt like the world had stopped and it was just the two of them left in motion. Every thought, every movement, every breath had been about Saana. And every time after, there'd been the lingering sensation of that moment in their kisses, making each touch of lips on lips a special occasion.

This time, though…

Oh, this time was like being thrown back to the very first kiss but with the sensations magnified by each instant they'd been apart.

They clung together, bodies still fitting perfectly despite her belly, and she hugged Saana as tightly as possible without hurting her, physical desire subsumed by emotional need.

It was ridiculous to pretend that when she'd made that headlong, fear-filled flight from Texas, it was simply to go to someone she trusted. No. She'd known, in her heart, that what she'd needed was Saana to hold her, to be with her through the crazy and leech the fear away.

When she was holding Saana, she felt unstoppable, able to face anything.

But this was her submissive girl, who needed to be coaxed and aroused until she forgot her need for control, so Kenzie broke the kiss and picked up the scrubby again. Then she slowly bathed Saana, using the otherwise mundane task as foreplay.

"Turn around, babe."

She made her voice strong, even while inside she was melting with desire.

Exhaling a shuddering breath, Saana did as bid, facing Kenzie but leaning on the wall like her legs didn't want to hold her up.

Slowly, Kenzie worked the suds over Saana's arms, then shoulders. Paying special attention to those firm, high breasts, circling until the already tight nipples contracted to dark points and Saana's breath rasped in her throat. Down to her belly, teasing now, skimming over flesh glowing rosy from her attention.

Then she started to stoop to wash her legs, and Saana held her shoulder, stopping her.

"My turn," she said, her voice gone husky and her eyes gleaming.

Kenzie made no argument. After all, she'd been longing to have her wife's hands all over her. And there was something absolutely soul-shaking to see the care with which Saana rubbed the soap across the bulge of Kenzie's belly, as if fascinated by it.

Then she looked up and said, "I never knew how beautiful a pregnant body could be until I saw yours."

Kenzie tried to chuckle, but her throat felt too tight to let the laughter through. Instead, she finally replied, "I'm glad you feel that way."

"I do." Saana's soapy hands were on either side of Kenzie's belly, moving in slow, tender circles. "I just about fell down in Maria's office when you took off your shirt and I saw the changes in your body. So sexy."

Her wife's words were melting away her restraint, and Kenzie gently took the sponge away from Saana and backed the other woman under the water to rinse off. Once she was sure Saana's back was soap free, Kenzie turned her to rinse her front. Lightly biting the nearest shoulder, Kenzie reached around to put her hand between Saana's thighs, and her wife's moan of pleasure made her arousal kick up a notch.

Wet heat enfolded her fingers, and the inner muscles contracted. Avoiding Saana's clitoris as best she could, Kenzie slowly pushed deeper inside, then pulled back out.

"I remember all the things you like, babe," she said against the damp nape. "And if you're a good girl, I'll do as many as you want."

"God, Kenzie." Saana had her hands flat against the wall, her entire body trembling, seemingly already on the brink of coming.

"Do you still have the toys I bought you?"

"Yes…"

It was a whispered groan, and Saana shuddered again as Kenzie pinched her nipple.

"I'm not using them tonight," Kenzie said. Saana had said no one had ever talked dirty to her until Kenzie and admitted it made her hot. "Tonight, I'm using my hands, and mouth, and tongue, and I'm gonna make you come until you tell me to stop."

Without waiting for a reply, she reached out and turned off the water, then tugged her wife out of the shower. Grabbing towels, they dried off hurriedly, and then they were kissing again, and Kenzie, unable to resist, pushed Saana up against the wall and gave her the first orgasm of the night.

"We didn't even make it to the bed," she said with a laugh as Saana sagged in her arms, trying to catch her breath. "Are you ready to go again?"

"You're so bad." Saana straightened, pushing her hair out of her blushing face.

"That doesn't answer my question."

Shaking her head, her face getting even rosier, Saana said, "Honestly? Yes. I'm always ready with you."

Giving her a hard kiss and taking her hand, Kenzie replied, "Good girl. Let's go and set that bed on fire."

And she was rewarded by her wife's huff of laughter as she led her into the bedroom.

She didn't want to think about the question

Saana had asked earlier—about what had gone wrong between them. Just thinking about it made the dark thoughts about her own unworthiness to be here with Saana rise up to strangle her self-respect.

So, instead of dwelling on them, Kenzie concentrated on her wife's pleasure.

Pulling Saana down onto the bed, Kenzie took her hands and guided them to the headboard.

"Hang on to that," she said, making it a demand. "When you want me to stop, let go and I'll stop."

It was a game they'd played before. One that had left them both aroused, then wild with lust.

"Kenzie…" It was just a sigh, but Kenzie's body tightened in anticipation.

She played Saana's body like a well-remembered instrument, finding and loving on all the places she knew would ratchet her wife's need higher and then higher still.

Then, as she kept her hovering just on the brink of release, Kenzie had a moment of déjà vu so strong she forgot to breathe.

Here, at this point, with Saana's shudders firing into her own flesh, making Kenzie almost come in sympathy, would be when she used to say, *Tell me you love me…*

The words hovering on her lips, she froze, the need to say them almost as strong as her desire. Saana's eyes were closed, her body bowed off the bed, trembling and jerking, obviously yearning for the final touch that would push her over into orgasm.

Tears flooded Kenzie's eyes, but she refused to let them fall. Instead, she eased Saana back and then, before her wife could respond, buried her head between Saana's thighs and sent her crying out over the edge.

And she kept her head there, wringing out another orgasm from Saana, until she was sure no evidence of her tears remained on her face.

CHAPTER TWELVE

SAANA WOKE UP on Sunday with the sun blazing in through a chink in her curtains and the unmistakable sensation of her world having been severely rocked.

They'd made love late into the night. Each time Saana thought she couldn't carry on a moment more, Kenzie would touch her or make some erotic demand that set her afire all over again.

Although she didn't agree that nothing had changed after their passionate night, she couldn't bring herself to regret it. Maybe Kenzie had been right about everything being easier if they got the physical out of their system.

Saana sat up and stretched, laughing ruefully at herself.

She'd never get Kenzie out of her system.

Kenzie had apparently woken up way ahead of her and already gone downstairs since her side of the bed was cold except for where Saana herself had been lying. After rushing to wash and dress, Saana made her way downstairs.

Not surprisingly, Kenzie was in the kitchen, which smelled deliciously of bacon and pancakes.

"Mornin'." Kenzie smiled over her shoulder, lush lips a sly, conspiratorial curve. "Sleep okay?"

"Like a log, when someone finally allowed me to go to sleep," she quipped in response, feeling her cheeks heat.

Kenzie chuckled and turned back to the stove, leaving Saana wondering if it would be appropriate to kiss her good morning. Then she mentally shrugged. She was as invested in the situation, in her own way. If she wanted to kiss her wife good morning, why shouldn't she?

And Kenzie didn't seem to object, since she curved her free hand around the nape of Saana's neck and held her in place for a kiss that made Saana's toes curl.

"Mmm…yeah. Really good mornin'," Kenzie murmured with another sly smile as Saana backed away. "By the way, your phone's been ringin' and pingin' for a while. Hopefully, it wasn't anythin' too important."

"Probably Mom," she said, looking around, wondering where she'd left the damn thing. "Do you have anything planned for today?"

"Not really. Although I thought I'd just lounge around. Maybe take a swim."

Heat trickled along Saana's spine as a memory of the two of them swimming together in the past surfaced.

"Is there something you need me to do?" Kenzie continued when Saana didn't reply.

"Oh, no. I just thought we could drive over to Orlando and find you an outfit for the gala. It's coming up fast, and I heard you at the clinic telling Shelley none of your clothes fit properly anymore."

Kenzie snorted. "Even if they did, I'm pretty sure I don't have anything appropriate for a gala." She turned off the stove before bringing the patter of pancakes and crispy bacon to the table. "So, yeah, if you want me to be there and not embarrass you, I guess we better look for somethin'."

Saana's mouth watered at the sight and scent of blueberry pancakes and bacon—two things she didn't often eat—and as she reached for her fork, she replied, "You wouldn't embarrass me, no matter what you wore."

Kenzie didn't answer, but when Saana looked up, she saw the skepticism on her face clearly.

"I mean it," she said. It felt a little like stepping into a minefield, but she couldn't help adding, "Do you think I care how you dress?"

Kenzie shrugged, but her gaze was searching

as she admitted, "The clothes were just a part of it. I always thought I had to fit in with your friends and family and knew I never did."

"I didn't realize you thought I was so shallow," she said slowly, in part hurt but, more importantly, feeling the conversation held an important clue to what had gone wrong before. "So whenever I offered to buy you anything, you were thinking I was trying to make you somehow more acceptable to the other people in my life?"

Kenzie still held her gaze, but her chin tilted up. "It's in the past, Saana. I'm not worried about all that now, so it doesn't really matter."

Saana nodded, wanting time to think it over before continuing the conversation, and she didn't object when Kenzie changed the subject.

Just as they finished breakfast, Saana's phone rang again, and she got up to grab it.

"Hey, Mom. How are you?"

"Fine, darling. Just fine. I was wondering if you and McKenzie would like to come for lunch. I have something I want to talk to you both about."

She knew if she told her mother they had just eaten breakfast, she'd want to know what they were doing getting up so late, and just the thought made Saana blush.

"Sorry, Mom. We're just about to head over to Orlando to do some shopping."

"Oh." The disappointment in her mother's

voice was marked. "That's fine. I just wanted to talk to you about the nursery. Have you done anything about it yet?"

The question gave Saana an emotional jolt, and she couldn't help her gaze flying to Kenzie's face. In response, her wife raised questioning eyebrows, and Saana shook her head reflexively.

"No, Mom. We really haven't made any firm decisions about it. What with work, you know, there hasn't been a lot of time."

"That's why I'm offering to help. I thought you could get the door into your grandfather's old dressing room—you know the one you had sealed off—reopened, and that would be perfect for the nursery. Right next door, for when they wake up in the night."

Kenzie was still looking askance, but Saana was strangely reluctant to clue her into what Mom was saying. Although, it was inevitable it would be brought up at a not-too-much later date.

"That sounds like a good idea. Let me talk to Kenzie and get back to you."

"That's fine, darling, but don't wait too long. With first babies, and twins too, you might not have as much time as you think."

When Saana hung up, Kenzie asked, "What's your mom have up her sleeve?"

It was said with a certain tone of fondness, but Saana still felt a little defensive as she replied, "She was asking about our plans for the nursery."

Kenzie's eyes widened. "Damn," she muttered, getting up abruptly and picking up the plates off the table.

Surprised, Saana followed her over to the sink. "What's the matter?"

Kenzie ran the hot water over the plates to wash off the maple syrup and didn't respond until after she'd turned the tap off. Then she turned, placing her back against the counter and crossing her arms.

"Honestly, I'm startin' to feel pretty guilty about your mom." She frowned and shook her head. "I never expected her to be so into this whole baby thing. I hate to think how she'll feel when I leave again."

Determined not to make a big deal out of it, Saana shrugged. "She'll get over it. She's been dropping hints about grandchildren for a while, so I should have known she'd be excited. I suppose I should have warned you."

Kenzie's brows knit for a moment and then she straightened and turned back to the sink.

"Well, nothin' to be done about it now. Any way we can hold her off on the nursery? Seems a shame to waste the money."

Saana's heart clenched, but she made her voice cool as she replied, "Money isn't an issue. And when you're ready to move on, you can take the furniture and everything with you so you don't have to worry about starting over from scratch."

"Kind of ya." Saana couldn't decide whether her tone was disgruntled or sarcastic. "But that's a bit more than I could accept."

"Well, then, how about you think of it as the best thing for your babies instead of immediately letting your pride lead the way?"

There was no mistaking the way Kenzie stiffened, but then she exhaled and her shoulders slumped.

"You're right. I'm being a brat and not thinking straight. But I need you to know…" Grabbing a towel, she faced Saana, drying her hands as she continued. "When I came here, I wasn't expecting to gain anything other than the custody of my babies. That was the only thing I was thinking about."

There was something so poignant about the way she said it that Saana couldn't help squeezing her shoulder and saying, "I know. If there's only one thing I know about you, I know you're not avaricious."

That seemed to strike Kenzie as funny, and she grinned. "I'd say you know a lot more about me than that…"

Saana found herself blushing again under that teasing gaze, and she quickly said, "Let's get ready and go to Orlando before it gets any later. If we get back early enough, we can still spend part of the afternoon in the pool."

Kenzie's laugh was frankly sensuous, and

Saana thought if her cheeks got any redder, they'd burn right off as her wife said, "I'm lookin' forward to that…"

They headed off to Orlando as soon as they'd gotten dressed, and Kenzie found herself more relaxed than she'd been in ages. The idea of Mrs. Ameri being excited about setting up a nursery for the babies still niggled at the back of her mind but couldn't dim the glow she'd gotten from the night before.

Adjusting her dark glasses, she leaned back in her seat and stretched her legs out as far as she could. Funny how, although she generally disliked shopping, she was looking forward to the trip with Saana. She'd only ever passed through Orlando, and Saana had suggested they go to the outdoor shopping-and-dining mall outside one of the theme parks for lunch. It would be more fun if they were going to the park to enjoy the rides, but there was no way Kenzie would do that with the babies on board.

Maybe one day, when they were older, she'd be able to take them for a vacation.

Somehow thoughts like that, which usually made her a little anxious about the future, today made her smile and feel hopeful.

"After our conversation this morning," Saana said suddenly as they were getting onto I-95 and she was merging with the traffic. "I was thinking you might want to consider staying in Florida once you get custody of the babies."

Kenzie sent Saana a sharp look, wondering why she'd suddenly come out with that.

"What're you suggestin'?"

"Just that you don't have any family back in Texas to be interested in your children when they're born. At least, that's what I've gathered from what you've said."

"With Aunt Lena gone, yeah, that's true." She wasn't close with any of her cousins, and in fact she had wondered whether it would be safe to move back into close proximity to Darryl's parents.

She shivered at the thought of them potentially kidnapping the babies and then berated herself for being silly.

"Well, then, it would make sense to stay fairly close by—not necessarily in Melbourne or on the East Coast—so that my parents can fulfil the grandparent role."

"Would they even want that?" she asked, really wondering *why* they might want to.

"I should think so." Saana sounded completely sure. "Besides, they already consider the babies mine as well as yours. Even though our relationship was rekindled only because of the legal problems, they don't know that."

Kenzie blew out a breath, not even ready to think about those particular complications coming about because of her need to protect her children.

"It isn't something you need to decide right now, but keep it in mind when it comes time to make any decisions."

"Sure."

But she knew staying close to Saana, having her in her life, wasn't something she wanted to have to deal with.

And she was glad when Saana dropped the subject.

When they got to the outdoor mall, Saana drew up to the curb, and a couple of valets came running up to open their doors. Kenzie swung her legs out and gratefully took the young man's hand so he could help her get out and to her feet.

Kenzie couldn't help laughing at herself. Any day now, she would get stuck in Saana's little sports car if she wasn't careful. Even her own larger, slightly higher sedan was becoming a chore to navigate. Besides, she really couldn't ask Saana to drive her old beater, with its finicky starter and questionable brakes, just because Kenzie had gotten so unwieldy.

Just imagining her elegant wife, who was casually used to the best of everything, even as a passenger in that decrepit old car made her grin again.

As they strolled into the first avenue between

the stores, Kenzie sniffed at the fragrant air. It even smelled expensive.

Best to get the situation straight from the get-go.

"Saana," she said quietly, not wanting to embarrass herself or her wife by being overheard. "I can't afford anything in here. You know that, don't you?"

That earned her a sideways glance, and her wife didn't even miss a step.

"I didn't expect you to buy anything," she replied. "I'm asking you to go with me to the gala, so I'm buying your outfit."

She didn't like it, but Kenzie knew that was for the best. It would be bad enough having to mingle with Saana's friends, without sticking out like a sore thumb because of what she was wearing.

"There's a shop along here that has maternity wear for all occasions, if I remember correctly." Saana turned down another wide avenue that ran at right angles to the first. "Ah, yes. Here it is."

The store was bright and light, with racks and racks of clothes, and Kenzie balked, stopping just inside the door.

"Go on," said Saana, resting a hand on the small of Kenzie's back and giving a little push. "Look around and see if there's anything you like. If not, there are other places we can try."

So Kenzie prowled around the store, trying to figure out which of the garments might suit her and not make her feel like a faker. After all, her usual dress code was either casual with a hint of cowboy, casual with a lot of hip-hop—like the shorts and tee she had on—or scrubs, none of which was represented in this chichi store.

Then, hanging on a wall, she saw a shimmery shirt with swirls of bronze and gold, and she paused to look closer at it.

Now that might work, if she could find some drapey pants to go with it. The only problem was that as she lifted one side of the front, she realized it was split from just below the bust. She'd seen pictures of expectant women wearing shirts like that, with their bellies on display, and wasn't sure she had that type of confidence, even if Saana declared it suitable.

"Is there something I can help you with?"

At the sound of the haughty voice behind her, Kenzie turned and met a pair of obviously scornful eyes.

"Yes," she said, emboldened and annoyed enough to try on the blouse she had just decided wouldn't work. "I'd like to try on this top."

The woman tilted her head, eyes artificially wide with fake innocence.

"That won't fit you. In fact, I'm quite sure nothing we have here will be in your size."

Funny how a few words combined with a certain attitude could take you right back and make you feel six years old again.

Six and small—not in physical size, but inside, where it really matters—making the comment hurt more than you had even imagined anything could.

Too small to do anything but walk away, knowing you were nothing but dirt—and cheap dirt, at that.

Then Kenzie looked across and saw Saana standing near the door, waiting for her, and everything inside rebelled against letting this sneering woman get the better of her.

Drawing herself up to her full height—only then realizing she'd unconsciously slumped—she stared down the woman.

"That's a shame," she said, letting her drawl deepen so the words dragged mockingly. "Do you work on commission?"

The woman hesitated, as if she didn't want to answer. Then she admitted, "I do."

Kenzie shook her head with pretend sorrow. "You've lost out today, then, girlie, since I guess my wife and I'll have to go somewhere else. We've got a fundraisin' gala to host and a mess of cash to spend, but definitely not in here."

"Did you see anything you like?" Saana had come up behind the saleswoman, and the woman turned quickly to see who was speaking.

"Afraid not, darlin'." Kenzie sent her wife a smile and then took her arm. "This ain't the place for us."

And she was so happy she could have cried when Saana didn't ask any questions but simply walked out beside her, their arms linked.

CHAPTER THIRTEEN

LIFE SETTLED INTO a routine after that first full week of Kenzie being back in Florida, with work, doctor's appointments, and visits to and from Saana's parents. Not terribly exciting on the surface, except for the nights spent together, making love whenever they could.

For the first time in memory, Saana found herself resenting how busy she was with work. It would have been nice to have more time with Kenzie, especially when she considered how short their time together probably would be. But because of their routine and new-found closeness, Saana found herself sinking into a lovely fantasy that this was how things would continue to be in the future.

Willful amnesia, she thought, if she thought about the situation at all.

However, it was easier to simply *not* think about it and just continue to drift through the days, enjoying Kenzie's company and the feeling that having her there made her house a home.

Mom had completely taken over the decoration of the nursery after intensive consultation with Kenzie.

"Darling," she said in that conspiratorial way she had, "it makes absolutely no sense to ask Saana what she'd like. Whenever I do that, she gives me the blankest look, as though she doesn't even know what paint *is*."

"She is rather more scientific than artistic," Kenzie had replied, sending Saana a teasing glance. "I do think, of the two of us, I'm the more imaginative."

Saana had immediately been transported back to their bed, images of some of their more adventurous sex-capades flashing into her brain. And she'd had to turn away so her mother wouldn't see her reddened cheeks.

"Any ideas on theme?" Thankfully, her mother had continued on, unaware of her daughter's randy thoughts. "We could do a jungle theme— I think that would be so pretty, and gender neutral too—or a fairy tale, although that's a little more difficult for a boy, I think. Or am I just being old-fashioned?"

"I think you're kinda right," Kenzie agreed. "When I think fairy tale, I imagine princesses and castles, although there are knights and dragons and stuff, too, huh?"

"Is there anything you're thinking of?" Mom asked, almost absentmindedly stroking the side of Kenzie's belly. It never failed to amaze Saana how enthralled her mom was with Kenzie's growing middle and how Kenzie put up with her ignoring the concept of personal space.

"Actually… I kinda do, but you might think it's dumb." Kenzie's gaze flicked back and forth between Saana and Mom.

"Tell me," Mom insisted. "I'm sure I can work with it."

"Well, I don't know if you knew this, but my great-grandmother was Native American, and I've always loved the Old West and native patterns and themes."

"Oh, yes." Mom had actually clapped her hands in excitement, making both Saana and Kenzie chuckle. "Leave it to me."

But, of course, she'd run every decision past Kenzie, and Saana again wondered about her wife's patience.

It would have driven Saana crazy.

By then she'd shown Kenzie the room, now used as a catch-all for luggage and whatnot, and the door to their bedroom next door.

"Back in the day, both husband and wife had separate dressing rooms," she explained. "But when I got the house, I converted what had been my grandmother's into the walk-in closet and closed off the door to my grandfather's since I didn't need the space. All I need to do is have a carpenter come and remove the drywall, and we'll have easy access to the babies once they move to the nursery."

"It's definitely big enough," Kenzie said, walking over to the curtains and opening them up. "And nice and bright too. But are you sure you want to go to all that trouble? It's not like it's on the other side of the house. I can walk out into the corridor and down the hall just fine."

Saana shrugged but smiled too.

"Hey, it won't take a lot to open the door up again, and it wouldn't take much to close it back off. I'm sure it would make it much easier for you after the babies are born and they're old enough to have their own space."

One Sunday, on a whim, they drove down to Vero Beach and walked around, had lunch, and then stopped at an outlet mall and bought two bassinets, along with a bunch of baby clothes. Kenzie kept saying they had enough things, but Saana, who'd never considered herself even remotely broody, couldn't help picking out one cute outfit or toy after another.

"You're a menace," Kenzie said as they left the store almost staggering under the weight of the bags. "Between your mom and you, y'all gonna spoil these babies."

"And what's wrong with that?" she couldn't help asking. "If I'm not mistaken, you're going to be a complete disciplinarian. These kids are going to need somebody to be on their side when you get going."

Kenzie had given her a sideways glance, as though trying to decide how to respond. Then she'd laughed and shaken her head, choosing to argue about which of them would be stricter rather than point out that Saana probably wouldn't be around to intercede on their behalf.

They'd been on a conference call with the lawyer in San Antonio, who'd advised them Darryl's parents seemed to be waiting for the babies to actually be born before they filed suit.

"It makes sense," she'd explained. "They'll want to have the names on the legal papers, rather than just 'infant child.' Besides, if anything were to happen to either McKenzie or the babies, their plans would certainly change."

"Are you sure they're even still planning to sue for custody? They might have changed their minds."

Hearing Kenzie ask that had been one of the few times over the last weeks that Saana had been forced to acknowledge that although she was enjoying their time together, Kenzie may not be. Not as much, at any rate.

"Unfortunately, I don't think there's much hope of that. And although I've offered mediation, they won't hear of it."

"I don't blame them," Kenzie had said fiercely. "I'm not willin' to negotiate with them over my children, so I'm not surprised they don't want to either!"

"Well, if I hear anything more, I'll contact you. And do let me know when the babies are born."

They'd hung up, and Kenzie huffed.

"I can't believe they're still pursuing this," she'd said. "I was hoping once they knew they'd have a fight on their hands, they'd give up."

Saana hadn't known what to say. They both knew Mr. and Mrs. Beauchamp wouldn't give up on the chance to raise their son's children now that they'd lost him. But each time Saana tried to work her way around to urging Kenzie to compromise, she'd been shot down.

Kenzie still wasn't in the mood to even contemplate it.

The day before the fundraising gala, while they were at work, Saana noticed Kenzie was moving a bit slower, and her smile was strained.

In between patients, she cornered her in the exam room.

"Are you okay?"

"Yeah," Kenzie said. "Just achy. I think I'm having Braxton-Hicks contractions."

Saana's heart leapt and then started to gallop.

"We should call Maria, see if she can take a look."

That made Kenzie chuckle.

"Saana, it's seven o'clock at night, and I'm quite sure it's nothing. If it gets worse, I'll ask

Dr. Preston to take a look to make sure, but I'm pretty certain it's false labor."

She hadn't been happy about it, but Saana had backed off, having to be content with keeping a sharp eye on Kenzie for the rest of the night.

Later, when they got home, they showered together, after which Saana rubbed Kenzie's belly with cocoa butter lotion, as she'd started doing each evening. It often turned into foreplay, but that evening, when Kenzie made it known she wanted to make love, Saana refused.

"You didn't sleep well last night," she said. "And the Braxton Hicks must be exhausting. Get some sleep, okay? We have some running up and down to do tomorrow before our hair and nail appointments and then a late night at the gala, and I know you never sleep past seven in the morning."

Kenzie lay back with a disappointed groan. "What does any of that have to do with us gettin' it on tonight? Our appointments aren't until midday. What else do you have going on?"

Saana made sure to turn her back so Kenzie couldn't see her expression because she knew it would give away at least a hint of her secret.

"I just need to pick up something I ordered," she said, making her voice unconcerned.

"Are you sure it's more important than giving your wife orgasms?" Kenzie asked in a teasing, enticing tone. "And getting a few yourself?"

But Saana wouldn't budge, even though her skin tingled and heat gathered in her belly at the thought.

Next morning, Saana had to exert all the control she could muster not to act like a giddy fool and alert Kenzie to the fact there was something other than the normal going on. Getting her wife into the car at ten was a chore since Kenzie was, by then, grousing about how early they were leaving home.

When they drove to Cocoa Beach and Saana turned into the car dealership, Kenzie didn't even look interested; she was probably thinking Saana was just having something on the car checked.

"You better come in with me," she told Kenzie as she turned off the ignition. "It's too hot for you to stay out here, and I don't want to leave the car running."

"Sure." Kenzie opened her door and swung her feet around, but by the time she was trying to lever herself out, Saana was there to give her a hand. "Damn, I'm like a beached whale. I might need to get a jack of some kind to hoist me in and out of vehicles soon."

Saana laughed and said, "I'll take the video so in the future, you can show the kids just what they reduced you to."

"Ha ha." But she was smiling as they walked through the door and into the lobby. "Yeah. I'm thinking I'll have enough ammunition to guilt trip them for the rest of their lives."

"Sit here and wait, if you want," Saana told her, still chuckling. "I won't be long."

Then she hurried over to the desk, too excited to wait even a moment more.

Kenzie watch Saana stride over the reception desk and wondered what was going on. She's been acting a little strange the last couple of days, and Kenzie couldn't put her finger on the source.

She wasn't sure whether to be worried or not.

Sometimes Saana was incredibly difficult to read. Kenzie didn't think she'd ever met someone so able to conceal their thoughts as effectively.

Sighing, rubbing at her back, she tried to find a comfortable position in the chair. Over the last few days, she'd become aware of a change in her body and, actually, her mental state too. The Braxton Hicks had surprised and scared her at first, but that was probably normal. The babies weren't due for another five weeks but—as everyone kept reminding her—with first babies and especially multiples, anything was possible.

In reality, she was mentally holding her breath until she passed her thirty-seventh week. Not that the babies wouldn't probably be healthy if they were born now at thirty-five, but the longer they stayed in her uterus, the better. All she'd ever wanted was for them to be healthy, and going to term was obviously the best outcome. However, she was quickly getting to the stage where she felt like she was floundering around, constantly overheated, either thirsty or needing to pee—sometimes both at the same time.

Now she completely understood women who said they were ready to give birth two or three months before their due date!

She looked up as Saana and one of the dealership employees walked toward her, but she didn't bother to get up, expecting them to go past her and out to Saana's car. Instead, they came straight over to her and stood, looking at her.

"Come on," Saana said.

"Oh, you're all finished?"

"Not quite, but you need to come with me."

"Ugh," she replied, sliding her butt to the edge of the seat, then using the armrests to get herself onto her feet. "Couldn't I just sit here until you're done?"

Saana just shook her head, her deadpan expression somehow annoying. "No."

Back out into the heat they went, Kenzie trailing behind the other two, not really paying attention, so that when Saana stopped abruptly, Kenzie almost ran into her.

"What do you think?" Saana waved her hand toward a sport utility vehicle parked in front of the building. "Do you like that color?"

Kenzie frowned at the high-end vehicle, wondering why she was even being asked about someone else's car. Then, knowing she was being a total grump but unable to help it, she said, "Nah. It's too bright a red. Looks trashy."

Saana shot her a strange look while the man with them made a sort of gurgling noise, as if he'd been throat punched.

"Really?" Saana asked, her eyes suddenly twinkling and her lips twitching, like she were trying not to laugh. "I thought that was your favorite color."

"It is," she said, wrinkling her nose. "But not on a car."

"Okay." Saana turned to the man beside her to ask, "That'll teach me to try to surprise my wife. What other colors do you have? But I want the same features we discussed last week."

"Um, I'll have to check, but it's a custom paint job. I don't know…"

Then, and only then, as Saana told the man in no uncertain terms that none of that mattered, did it come home to Kenzie what was going on, and she felt her knees get weak.

"Saana, wha…?"

"I bought this car for you." She said it casually, glancing over then quickly coming to put her arm around Kenzie's waist. "Are you all right?"

"You… You bought this? For me?"

Kenzie suspected her wife would have shrugged if her shoulder wasn't being used to prop her up.

"You can hardly get in and out of either of the cars, and when the babies are born, you're going to need a vehicle that can accommodate two car seats with ease, so yes. I bought this for you. But if you hate it, we can get something else—"

"Are you kiddin'?" Kenzie knew she was shouting but didn't care. "I love it! Don't you dare change a damn thing!"

And it was only later she realized she hadn't even balked for a second at the expense of the gift or thought about being beholden to Saana even more than she already was.

Instead, what came to mind was how considerate and wonderful the woman she married really was and how much she loved her for it.

But while in the past she'd have thought those emotions injurious to her own peace of mind, just then she couldn't work up the strength to care.

CHAPTER FOURTEEN

THE EVENING OF the gala was warm and muggy, making Kenzie glad her top was sleeveless and had a deep V-neck, and her pants were almost gossamer-fine silk. She was even more pleased to find out that instead of being held outside in the Ameris' extensive and beautiful gardens, they'd set everything up indoors.

"I wanted to wait until later in the year," Saana's mom had said to Kenzie a couple of weeks earlier. "Then it would be cooler, and all our friends from up north would be here for the winter. But getting the trust and the work Saana's doing in front of people's eyes as soon as possible was so important we decided to do this now."

Taking out the necklace that was the only thing she'd inherited from Aunt Lena, Kenzie slipped her wedding ring onto it and then put it on, adjusting the band and heart pendant so they lay nicely in her cleavage. She'd tried to put the ring on, but it no longer fit.

Looking at herself in the mirror, Kenzie frowned.

She didn't look very much like herself, and it wasn't just because of her pregnancy. Her hair had been cut and styled in an expensive salon, and the mani-pedi she'd gotten had almost put her into a coma of pleasure. The clothes and shoes she was wearing cost more than a months' pay and made her feel guilty, even as she ran an appreciative hand over the sleek gold fabric of her blouse.

When she'd asked Saana if she'd be expected to wear makeup, her wife shrugged.

"That's totally up to you," she'd replied. "If you don't want to, then don't. You don't need it."

A comment that made her tingle with pleasure, even as it annoyed her as well.

She'd met a few of Saana's friends when she first came to live at the mansion, and they'd all looked at Kenzie like she'd crawled out of the bottom of a pond. Mind you, they'd made sure Saana wasn't aware of that, the hypocrites. Obviously, staying on Saana's good side had been first and foremost on their agenda. But a few times, as if realizing Kenzie wouldn't rat them out, they'd made their snide remarks when Saana was out of earshot.

"Where on earth did Saana dig you up? Vegas? Somehow, I'm not surprised."

"You're from Texas? Are you legal?"

"Do you have indoor plumbing where you're from?"

Just rude, stupid comments that made Kenzie feel like poop on the bottom of someone's shoe, even as she held her chin up and gave them the stink eye.

The image looking back at her from the mirror was nothing like the usual board shorts–wearing, flip-flop-loving woman she knew herself to be. In fact, she almost felt she was inside someone else's skin. A skin she needed to be able to get through the night without embarrassing Saana and her parents, or damaging the Preston Trust.

"Hey, are you ready?" Saana called from the walk-in closet. "Can you zip me up, please?"

Somehow the sound of Saana's slightly harried voice eased the band of anxiety around Kenzie's chest, and she said, as she walked over to the door, "You're gonna make us late, as usual."

Then, as she stepped into the closet, she halted, her heart turning over and desire flashing out to flood her veins.

Saana's dress was a simple column of coral silk that draped her body like a second skin, except where it flowed in soft pleats from one shoulder, across her bare back to the opposite hip. It hugged every curve and dip, bringing to Kenzie's suddenly feverish brain images of the sinuous, sexy way Saana moved as her arousal climbed, threatening to peak.

"Dear lord," she murmured, moving closer so as to run her palm across that bare, warm skin, tracing the line of her wife's vertebrae, feeling goose bumps fire up beneath her fingers. "How am I gonna keep my hands off you all evening? This is the sexiest dress in the world, and all I wanna do is take it off you."

Saana's blush made Kenzie lick her bottom lip, and her wife's cheeks turned even pinker.

"Stop that," she muttered, trying and failing to wrestle with the zipper at the side of her dress. "Now you're the one who's going to make us late, and don't think I won't blame you for it. Mom likes you better than me, anyway, so I'll happily throw you under the bus to avoid her fussing at me."

"Mm-hmm," Kenzie replied sarcastically, still wondering if they had time for one quick sexual encounter before the party. Nah. Unfortunately. She batted at Saana's hand. "Lift your arm. Let me do you up."

When Saana obeyed, Kenzie bent quickly to place a kiss right on the exposed edge of her wife's breast, eliciting a soft gasp. Then, before she changed her mind, she pulled up the zipper, tucking the tiny tab into the bodice so it became invisible.

"There," she said, unable to resist giving that truly wonderful ass a quick squeeze too. "Are you all ready to go? Your mom gave us strict instructions to be there by six thirty, and it's almost six now."

"Yes." God, that husky note in Saana's voice got her every time. "I'm ready."

"Me too," she replied, knowing Saana understood the double meaning when another wave of pink flooded her face. "But we have to go."

"Wait." Saana's voice, with its sharp edge, stopped Kenzie in her tracks. "Is that your wedding ring?"

Reaching up, Kenzie lifted it and nodded. "Yeah. I wanted to wear it tonight but couldn't get it on my sausage finger."

And although Saana didn't say anything more, her smile was all Kenzie needed.

"Oh, earrings!" Saana exclaimed, turning back into the closet abruptly. "Mom says no outfit is finished without some."

In two twos, she was back, fastening gleaming diamond drops to her earlobes as she quickstepped into the hallway.

Kenzie suppressed a grin. When they'd first met, she'd thought Saana was just one of those people who always walked fast—in a rush to get to where they were going. It was only later on she realized that her wife's speed had more to do with her constant lateness than anything else.

Climbing into the SUV, Kenzie said, "Have I adequately thanked you for buying this? It's so much easier to get into and out of than the cars. That automatic drop-down step is the bomb."

"It was this or a crane," Saana teased. "And I thought this would be more useful in the long run."

Laughing, Kenzie had to agree.

When they got to her parents' house, Saana drove around to the back entrance, where a guard let them in so they could park near the stand-alone garage. Inside the house, it was a hive of activity, with Mrs. Ameri and the party planner like army generals in the middle. When Mrs. Ameri saw them, she bustled over.

"There you are!" They both were hugged and received air-kisses, so as to avoid the spread of unwanted lipstick, Kenzie suspected. "Just in time to start greeting guests. Saana, that color looks lovely on you, and McKenzie, you're absolutely glowing. Gold suits you. You look like a Renaissance portrait."

She rushed off again, leaving Kenzie to ask, "Was that a compliment?"

Saana laughed, threading her arm through Kenzie's and leading her toward the great room at the back of the house, where a band was already playing.

"Yes, it was. You look fabulous. I've told you, pregnancy suits you."

Then there was an influx of guests needing attention. Saana kept her arm through Kenzie's for

a while as she greeted them—mostly by name—
and introduced everyone to Kenzie. They'd been
there for about forty-five minutes when Saana let
go to hug someone she called Uncle George, and
Kenzie eased away. When she realized Saana
hadn't noticed, she took another step back, then
another, until she could unobtrusively set off to
find a quiet place away from the limelight surrounding her wife.

"Is everything all right, McKenzie?"

At the sound of Mr. Ameri's voice, Kenzie
started guiltily.

"Yes. Sure. I just wanted to sit down for a
moment. My back's been sore the last couple
of days." His look of concern had her quickly
reassuring him that it wasn't anything serious.

"Ah, good." He looked around and then guided
her toward a table near the front of the room.
"Let me get you seated and get you something
to drink. Knowing Mariella, the cocktail hour
will be brought to a close exactly at eight, and
dinner will be announced." He sent his wife a
fond glance, before continuing, "She's a marti-
net when it comes to hosting these affairs. Posi-
tively frightening."

With a wink, he left her as Kenzie laughed
quietly. Even though she had no idea what a mar-
tinet was, she could make a pretty good guess,
having seen Mrs. Ameri keep everyone around
her on their toes.

And, just as he'd predicted, in fifteen minutes—at eight exactly—Mrs. Ameri announced that dinner would be served and asked everyone to take their seats.

"There you are," Saana said as she slid into one of the remaining seats at the table. "I wondered where you'd run off to."

She was glowing, and Kenzie felt her heart turn over as she was the recipient of that beautiful smile.

"Sorry. Had to get off my feet for a while. I know I should have been mingling, but—"

"No worries," was all she had time to say before her parents and two other couples interrupted by coming to take their seats.

Dinner was sumptuous, but Kenzie merely picked at her food, more worried about her table manners not being up to par than about eating. The conversation swirled around her, but it wasn't about anything she could comment on or contribute to, and the old self-conscious feelings started creeping up on her again.

"Have you been to Paris, McKenzie?" Mrs. Guilder suddenly asked, surprising her so much Kenzie almost choked on her food.

It seemed there was a general lull in the conversation because it felt as if everyone at the table was suddenly looking at her, and heat gathered at the back of Kenzie's neck.

She didn't dare look at Saana or her parents,

and for a long moment, she had no idea what to say. This was just the sort of thing she'd tried to avoid—to warn Saana about—but here she was anyway, on the spot and in the fire.

Well, then, to hell with it.

"No, ma'am," she said, rolling the drawl out like a rug. "Haven't been anywhere much and never outside of the States."

There was a choking sound from somewhere in Mr. Ameri's direction, but Kenzie kept her gaze fixed on Mrs. Guilder, who looked almost comically startled.

In for a penny, in for a pound.

"My parents both had substance abuse problems, so I was pretty much homeless until I was six. Then my mother was incarcerated, my father disappeared. My aunt took me in, although she already had three kids of her own. I was an orphan by the time I was ten, but I think I was damned lucky because I still had Aunt Lena givin' me a roof over my head and makin' sure I had food to eat."

Everyone at the table was listening now, and Kenzie had never felt more inferior in her life— surround by the wealthy, with their total lack of understanding of reality. But it was no use stopping now. Better to at least make her sad, sordid tale relevant to why they were supposedly all here and regain some semblance of pride.

Firming her lips, which felt like they may be

about to tremble, she lifted her chin and looked around the table at everyone except Saana.

She didn't want to see her wife's reaction to her words.

Her bad behavior.

"Which is why I'm so proud to be a part of the Preston Medical Clinic staff. I know what it's like to be without a home, insurance and medical care. My aunt told me that when my father dropped me off at her home after my mom went to jail, just before he disappeared, I was so sick she wasn't sure I'd make it."

Once more, she let her gaze wander around the table, and this time she forced herself to look at Saana. Her face was still, unmoving, but the expression in her eyes—a burning, angry look— made Kenzie's stomach fall.

But she'd started something Kenzie knew she had to finish, so she took a deep breath and continued.

"Turned out I had viral meningitis, and if Aunt Lena hadn't taken me to the emergency room, I'd have probably died. But the cost of the treatment and the hospitalization was something she couldn't afford and had to pay back over a very long time. That's not right, ya know? To have her kindness be so costly that when her own daughter got cancer, it almost bankrupted her. That's why we need places like Preston Medical."

Her hands were trembling by the time she'd

finished, so she kept them under the table, where they couldn't be seen, trying to keep her defiance at the forefront. Hoping all any of them would see was her dignity, not her fear.

"Well said, McKenzie." Surprisingly, it was Mrs. Guilder who spoke, and when Kenzie looked at her, she was nodding. "And please forgive me for putting you on the spot with my question. Of everyone here, I should have known better. We do like to pretend we've all grown up wealthy, and of course, some have, but I come from a hardscrabble town in Oklahoma, and if I hadn't met and married Myron, I'd probably still be a waitress, hardly able to make ends meet."

"Someone would have snatched you up," her husband said, taking her hand and kissing the back. "I'm just glad I saw you first."

And the conversation turned to the clinic and what else Saana wanted to achieve through the trust, but although Kenzie was brought into the conversation, she again avoided looking at Saana.

It was hard not to think her revelation, in front of all these people, hadn't caused a shift—perhaps even a break—in their relationship.

Kenzie had always avoided talking about her parents; there didn't seem to be anything to gain from bringing them up. To her, her life had started and been saved the night Aunt Lena took her in.

No one would have blamed her if she'd turned

her sister's no-good husband away and told him to take his child with him. Lena had been widowed just two or so years before, and although her husband had a small life insurance policy when he died, it had only been enough to bury him and pay off a portion of the mortgage.

One more mouth to feed had been the last thing she'd needed.

Thank goodness she hadn't thought that way.

Without her, Kenzie didn't know where she'd be.

What—who—she would have ended up as.

The rest of the evening passed in a bit of a blur. Feeling emotional wasn't one of Kenzie's favorite moods. It was exhausting. But although she longed to go home, she knew Saana had to stay to the end.

Thank goodness for Mrs. Ameri, who ushered the last of the crowd out the door at half-past eleven on the dot.

"I think that was a resounding success," she said happily as they sat together in the den, while the catering staff finished cleaning up. "I'm looking forward to hearing the total donations tomorrow, but according to Jean, everyone was very generous."

"Thank you, Mom." Saana got up and crossed the room to kiss her mother on both cheeks. "We couldn't have done it without you."

The fondness in Mariella Ameri's smile as

she looked at her daughter made Kenzie have to blink back tears.

"You're very welcome, darling. I'm so very proud of you and all you're doing. But I think you should take poor Kenzie home. She looks exhausted."

Saana gave Kenzie what she could only interpret as a brooding look and nodded. "Yes, we should go."

And so, after saying goodnight to the Ameris, they went.

CHAPTER FIFTEEN

SAANA WASN'T SURE how to approach the subject of Kenzie's revelations during dinner.

At first, as she'd spoken, Saana had felt hurt that she was hearing this story for the first time, along with people who were little better than strangers to her wife.

Why hadn't Kenzie told Saana about her early life? Was it a matter of trust—or, more precisely, lack thereof?

In all the time Saana had known Kenzie, the only person who'd she'd ever spoken about in a parental role was her aunt Lena. Although she'd been very young when her aunt had taken her in, did she remember being with her parents? What had she seen? Experienced?

Had that time in her life left scars that maybe even Kenzie wasn't aware of but that had contributed to her extreme independence?

What else had it caused?

All those questions were flying through her

mind, but Kenzie looked so exhausted that Saana hesitated to bring it up.

"I'm sorry I embarrassed you earlier."

Kenzie's voice surprised Saana out of her reverie, but she didn't sound terribly sorry, rather more defensive. Saana shot her wife a quick glance, and seeing her chin at that combative angle for some reason made her heart ache.

"You didn't," she said softly, trying to gauge how best to proceed.

"Then why were you so angry?"

"I wasn't angry."

Yet even as she said it, she knew it wasn't true.

Clearly, Kenzie did, too, because she snorted rudely.

"What does that sound mean?" Saana asked, unable to rein in her own annoyance.

"I'm trying to figure out whether you're lying to me or yourself. I know you well enough to know when you're angry."

"I was shocked to hear your story, McKenzie, and—"

Kenzie snorted again, interrupting her. "You weren't shocked. You were definitely angry. You're still angry. You only call me McKenzie when you are."

That was, in Saana's mind, a step too far.

"Don't you dare tell me what I felt or thought." She couldn't help the coolness of her tone, and from the corner of her eye, she saw Kenzie turn to look at her. "I was angry because of what you went through and, if you want the entire truth, because you seemed willing to tell the story to strangers but had never told *me*."

"Maybe because I didn't want to." The words were like a dart through Saana's heart. "Because I don't want your sympathy or to be looked at as a victim of my parents' bad choices. That has *nothing* to do with who I am."

"I know that." Saana said it although she didn't really mean it. The weight of love sitting directly on her heart made her want to cry. "But it's a part of you—your history—and I'd have liked to hear it from you, in private, rather than in front of everyone else."

"Sorry." It was grudgingly said, but Saana's anger faded.

"It's okay. I understand why you'd feel that way."

"Thanks. I appreciate you sayin' so."

Kenzie yawned, turning her head to the side, looking out the window, and after a few moments of silence, Saana realized her wife had fallen asleep.

Sighing, Saana turned the conversation over in her head.

Now that she knew what Kenzie had gone through, she was forced to look at her own reactions to her wife's behavior.

If she were honest, early in their marriage,

she'd been unable to understand why Kenzie, at her age, was still studying to become a nurse. There were grants, and scholarships, and loans she could have taken out, allowing her to go to college and finish quickly rather than have it take forever and a day. As much as she'd loved her, Saana acknowledged now that she'd also judged her without having the first idea of why she was the way she was.

Saana had even found herself getting annoyed at the way Kenzie wouldn't accept the help, particularly the financial assistance, she offered. After all, Saana was rich and a doctor. Any normal woman would be pleased to be with someone who not only had the means to give them whatever they wanted but also was generously willing to do so.

Wow. Thinking about it now, in light of her new understanding, Saana actually felt ashamed. And incredibly proud of all Kenzie had been able to achieve.

Having pulled into the garage, Saana turned off the ignition and gently shook Kenzie awake. When her eyes opened, she looked around, seemingly disoriented.

"We're home." Saana's kept her voice as soft as the hand that skimmed Kenzie's cheek. "You're going to have to awake up. Unfortunately, I can't carry you inside."

Kenzie chuckled, seemingly having put their

argument behind her. Rubbing her eyes, she straightened from her sideways slump.

"You'd definitely hurt yourself if you tried," she replied, taking off the seat belt after Saana unlatched it. "Let's keep it that only one of us has a backache, okay?"

As they meandered slowly into the house, Saana was left wondering if Kenzie would accept or resent the new, tender feelings growing ever stronger in her wife's heart. Things had been so good between them Saana was truly reluctant to even try to find out.

She already knew that Kenzie wouldn't hesitate to take off if she didn't like the way things were heading, although Saana didn't know, really, why she'd run in the first place. That, too, would take some thinking about, in light of these new revelations—Kenzie's childhood, what she'd said earlier about trying to fit in, in particular.

Kenzie undressed and fell into bed while Saana was still taking off her makeup, and although Saana was tired, too, she found herself lying in the dark, still thinking about the evening. Kenzie had spoken her truth with more than a hint of defiance, daring those listening to judge her life or look down on her experience.

Instead, it had filled Saana with helpless rage as she listened to Kenzie talk about her parents, and also pride at the resilience of the woman she loved so dearly.

And it was the sense of pride that had her rolling over to spoon around Kenzie's back and finally fall asleep.

She was dreaming. One of those dreams you know is a dream and yet seems incredibly real.

They were standing on the Eiffel Tower, Kenzie and she. Not on the observation deck but literally on the Eiffel Tower. Outside, being buffeted by the wind, hanging on to a pole or antenna.

"We need to get down," she shouted to Kenzie. "It's too dangerous. You might fall."

Kenzie tilted her head, as though unable to hear what Saana had said, and shouted something back.

Saana couldn't hear her either.

Looking around, she tried to find the way down, but there were no steps or lifts, nothing to indicate how they'd gotten up there in the first place. Desperate now, her heart pounding, she tried to stoop down, hanging on to the pole for balance, thinking that if she did, the change in perspective might show her where to go.

From the corner of her eye, she saw Kenzie move. When she looked around, she instinctively screamed, seeing her wife had let go of the antenna, the only thing keeping her tethered. She was being pushed backward by the wind, about to go over the edge—

Jolting awake, Saana lay panting, trying to

determine if she was still dreaming or actually awake.

"Saana." Kenzie's voice came to her out of the dark. "Saana, it's all right."

Was it? Would it ever be again?

"I… I'm okay."

"You were dreamin', babe. Sounded like a bad one." A hand, soft and soothing, stroked her shoulder, then her hair. "You shouted."

Swallowing her fear, she composed her voice to calmness.

"I'm sorry I woke you."

Kenzie made a rude noise that made Saana smile, even though her heart was still hammering.

"Don't worry about it."

"Go back to sleep, Kenzie. I'm okay."

But Kenzie's hand drifted to her throat, lingered there, fingers finding and measuring her pulse.

"Your heart's racing and not in a good way." Her lips replaced her fingers, and the wet heat of her tongue fired goose bumps over what felt like every inch of Saana's skin. "I won't promise to calm you down, but you'll be excited in a far better way."

Saana wanted to object, to say Kenzie needed her sleep, but they were kissing, and every other thought, every other concern, fled her mind.

All she felt were those full, sensual lips on

hers, the wet, slick slide of their tongues against each other.

With Kenzie, Saana's need didn't build slowly. Instead, it flamed instantly, ignited by her wife's touch, her kisses, the sound of her voice demanding complicity. And in its path was all Saana's fears and inhibitions, incinerated.

Some nights, Kenzie demanded Saana give her pleasure, with the promise of ecstasy returned two-, three-, fourfold. On others, like this night, Kenzie caressed and kissed and aroused Saana into a sensual stupor, holding her there.

"Open wider."

Her legs fell to the sides as if the words were strings and she were a marionette. Those fingers, long and strong and oh so knowledgeable, slid home, stroking through the wetness of arousal, finding a spot deep inside that, until her, had been secret. Kenzie had found it, as sure as a musician finding the right note, and had learned how to play it until Saana arched, and strained, and craved orgasm more than air.

"Relax." Kenzie's voice was passion-rough, her fingers equally so, both combining to push Saana incrementally closer to the edge. "You're almost there, baby. Relax. Let me get you there."

She stroked faster, a little harder.

Just right.

Perfect.

Perfect.

Ahh…

As her body convulsed, she bit her lip to stay silent. To stop the words of love filling her heart from coming out.

Coming down off the high, she suddenly realized something was wrong. Instead of cuddling up close to her still, Kenzie was sitting on the side of the bed, barely visible in the darkness.

"Kenz?"

There was no immediate answer. Saana rolled onto her knees so as to put her hand on Kenzie's back. The muscles were rigid, shivering slightly. Then Saana felt her take a deep breath.

"I think I'm in labor."

They'd been warned about it, but Saana wondered if, like her, Kenzie had put the thought of premature labor out of her mind.

"African American women, women who've had IVF and women carrying multiples are all at risk of premature births," Maria Ramcharam had reminded them. "And of course, McKenzie is in all of those high-risk groups. As soon as you have any thoughts that you might be in labor, I need you to contact me and head to the hospital."

So that's what they did.

It was three in the morning when Saana helped Kenzie out of the SUV outside emerge, where they were met by an orderly with a wheelchair. Only years of practice keeping a cool head during emergencies carried Saana through with any kind of dignity. What she really wanted to do was abandon the vehicle right where it was and rush into the hospital with Kenzie.

As though knowing that, her wife looked back over her shoulder and blew Saana a saucy kiss.

Driving way too fast for a parking lot, she parked the car and dashed into the hospital.

And the waiting—and the extreme stress—began.

A nurse practitioner examined Kenzie and declared she was five centimeters. As Saana was helping her get comfortable, adjusting her pillows, promising to find the fluffy socks to warm up her feet, Kenzie grabbed her wrist and let out a curse.

"Water just broke," she said when the contraction had passed.

At five o'clock, Saana called her parents to let them know what was happening. By then Kenzie had only progressed to seven centimeters, and both she and Saana were watching the babies' heartbeats anxiously.

"It's too early. Too soon for them to come now," Kenzie kept saying.

"You're almost thirty-six weeks." Saana was trying to reassure her, even in the face of her own fear. "They'll be fine."

But there was no denying the fact they were both scared stiff.

At seven, Maria Ramcharam arrived, having been kept apprised of Kenzie's condition and wanting to check on it herself.

At that point, with each contraction, one baby's heart rate slowed dramatically, and although it picked back up when the contractions passed, Maria suggested they err on the side of caution.

"I'm recommending you have a Caesarean section, but because you opted not to have an epidural or spinal block, we're going to have to do it under general anesthesia."

Kenzie immediately agreed, and Maria left the room to arrange for the operating room.

One of the nurses bustled around for a while and then left the room. As soon as they were alone, Kenzie grabbed Saana's wrist.

"I need to ask you a favor. A huge favor."

"Another one?" she asked, trying to keep it light, not liking how serious Kenzie looked.

"I'm serious."

"I think by now you know I'd do pretty much anything for you."

"If anythin' happens to me, I want you to keep the babies."

"Kenzie—"

"I mean it. I don't care if you let the Beauchamps see them or not, but I want you to raise them. If you do that, you can tell them about me, and they'll know I loved them and fought for them and *wanted* them so very much. If you give them to their grandparents, no matter what happens, they'll always feel deserted. Abandoned by the people who gave them life."

Saana swallowed, unable to stop the tears filling her eyes, and nodded.

"I'll do it, but nothing's going to happen to you, Kenzie. You'll be okay, and then you're going to feel silly even asking me."

"Doesn't matter," she said, shaking her head. "I don't care if I look like a fool right now. It's a parent's responsibility to try and cover the bases so as to protect their children. That's what I'm tryin' to do."

The nurse came back in just then.

"We going to move you now to prep you for surgery. You're going to have to wait in the surgical waiting area, Dr. Ameri."

Then another nurse came in with forms to be signed, and Saana knew she couldn't take the chance of losing Kenzie without telling her how she felt one last time.

But another contraction hit just then, and the chance to say she loved her passed before the words could be uttered.

"Dr. Amari…"

"Yes. I'm going."

Then, with one last look at first her wife and then the monitor, she swiftly left the room.

In the corridor, just standing there, unnerved and more frightened than she'd ever been before, she waited, wanting to see Kenzie go by before making her way to the surgical area of the hospital.

"Saana."

Her mother's voice jolted her out of her funk, and she turned to see her parents coming toward her, almost identical expressions of concern on their faces.

Then the door opened, and Kenzie was wheeled out.

"McKenzie."

Mom and Dad reached out, touching her hand and arm as the nurses wheeled her by, and Kenzie smiled a slightly lopsided smile and called out, "Thanks for being here. Take care of your daughter. She looks a little pale."

As the love of her life disappeared down the hallway, all of a sudden, a thought crossed Saana's mind, and she pushed past her parents to go after the gurney.

"Kenzie. The names."

But it was too late. They'd already turned into the elevator, and the doors had closed, leaving Saana a trembling, terrified mess.

CHAPTER SIXTEEN

SHE NAMED THEM Leanna and Darren.

"Leanna was Aunt Lena's given name," she told Saana late on the evening she'd given birth, after she'd come out of the anesthetic. "And Darren because I prefer it to Darryl."

"Makes perfect sense," Saana replied, her gaze stuck like glue to Leanna and Darren, who were both asleep on Kenzie's chest.

They'd been born without complications—Leanne at six pounds, four ounces and Darren at seven pounds flat—but Maria Ramcharam had said she'd be keeping Kenzie in the hospital for four days, worried about the chance of an embolism. Leanne had a touch of jaundice and had spent part of the first day in the NICU.

In Kenzie's mind, they were the most beautiful babies in the world, although she suspected every mother thought the same thing. Her only regret was having been out of it when they were born.

"I can't believe you got to hold them before

I did," she groused, looking up in time to see Saana smile.

"I didn't, really," Saana replied. "You held them for almost nine months."

Darren wriggled, his eyes opening a crack, but then went back to sleep.

Kenzie wished they would wake up, although she knew she'd probably look back on that thought and laugh at its craziness sometime in the future.

"Mom and Dad were asking if they could come by during visiting hours to see you all."

The way Saana stroked a gentle finger down each baby's cheek in turn threatened to completely melt Kenzie's heart.

"Your parents are welcome anytime. You know that."

Glancing up, Saana grinned suddenly, replying, "You might not want to tell them that. We might go home tomorrow and find them living in our house."

Kenzie chuckled with her, then shifted slightly, trying to ease a sudden muscle cramp in her arm.

"Can I take one of them for you?"

"Sure," Kenzie said on a yawn.

Perching on the edge of the bed, Saana expertly lifted Darren and cradled him in one arm, looking down to coo at him, "Who's the sweetest little man who ever was, hmm?"

Then she glanced up, meeting Kenzie's gaze,

and there was no mistaking the way the shutters came down over her face, making Kenzie's heart give a little jolt.

"I think we should hyphenate the babies' last names. If Darryl's parents are waiting to get word of their birth, it would probably be wise to give them a firm indication that you're not fighting them alone. If they're the kind of people who like to know what they're up against, they'll investigate, hopefully finding out the Ameris aren't going to just roll over to their demands."

There was that cool tone, which told Kenzie there was something being hidden. With Saana, it usually meant some unwanted or secret emotion, but that couldn't be the case here. Perhaps she just wanted to sound businesslike—in fact, removing the emotion from the discussion altogether?

"I'll think about it," she said with another yawn. "But I can't wrap my brain about what else that would mean right now."

"What else it would mean?"

"Yeah. The consequences for all of us, you know?"

Just then, Leanna let out a wail that seemed so completely out of proportion to her size that it startled her mama into laughter.

"Maybe she's ready to eat? Leanna, please don't wake up your brother. I haven't got this whole breastfeeding thing down yet, and I don't think I can handle both of you at the same time."

"Relax, babe. It'll be fine. And if it doesn't work, that's why we have bottles."

The words, so warm and understanding, made her tear up a little. During her obstetrics rotation, she'd seen so many new mothers driven to anxiety attacks because they couldn't get their babies to nurse, and no one offered the right support.

"One of the nurses said to call her when it was time. Can you ring the bell for me?"

Saana did as she was asked and then, apparently thinking Kenzie might not like her hovering, moved over to the visitor's chair on the other side of the room.

Intellectually, Kenzie had known she may have issues breastfeeding, but by the time she finally got Leanna latched on and had gotten over the rush of painful pins and needles, she was frazzled.

And as soon as the nurse left the room, Darren started fussing.

"You could probably tandem feed." Saana was bouncing Darren, trying to keep him calm. "Should I call the nurse back?"

Close to tears, Kenzie shook her head. How she hated seeing—feeling—so weak.

"No. Maybe you should go and get him a bottle." There was no way she could handle any more right then, with her incision making it impossible to shift positions and Leanna, just then, losing her grip on the nipple.

Kenzie cursed and started to cry, adding her sobs to both babies' wails.

"Aw, babe." Saana came over, and although her words were tender, her tone brooked no argument. "I'm going to tell the nurse to bring two bottles, okay—but in the meantime..."

Kenzie didn't even realize what Saana was doing until she found herself with Leanna back on the breast but now lying on a pillow, her body curled back, almost under Kenzie's arm. And she made no objection when Saana positioned Darren the same way on the other side, tickling his tiny mouth with her nipple and guiding his head until, miraculously, he, too, latched on.

"Will you be okay while I go and get the bottles?"

Kenzie snorted, unable to laugh because her nose was stuffy, and she was afraid to cough because of the pain. She'd need someone to press the pillow into her middle, and all pillows were otherwise in use just then.

"I think it's clear I don't need them anymore. Why did I bother with the nurse when you've proven to be just as efficient?"

Saana shrugged. "I just hate to see you upset and not do anything about it." She glanced toward the door and asked, "Will you be okay for a little? I want to go and head Mom and Dad off at the pass until you've finished breastfeeding."

"Sure. I'm all right just now." A jolt of anxiety made her add, "But don't be long, okay?"

And when Saana replied, "I won't be. I promise," Kenzie felt herself relax.

Saana called her parents and asked them to wait at least half an hour before leaving to come to the hospital. Then, when the babies finished feeding, Saana offered to take one of them for the recommended fifteen minutes of skin-to-skin bonding and was thrilled when Kenzie agreed.

"I was wonderin' how I was goin' to manage both of them," she said. "The nurse just made it sound so easy. 'Remember to spend time cuddling your babies after feeding.' I want to, but right now I'm a little overwhelmed."

"Understandable. I'm feeling a bit that way myself, and I didn't have a C-section this morning."

Laying Leanna down in the cot for a moment, Saana undressed to the waist, subduing her natural shyness about public nudity. This was, after all, a special and important circumstance. Rolling the cot over to the comfortable chair beside the door, glad that she'd insisted on a private room, she sat down to unswaddle the baby.

The sensation of that soft, fragile life against her chest made all the air leave her lungs in a rush, and the wave of tenderness that crashed through her made tears fill her eyes. When she tucked the blanket around them both and Leanna relaxed into a sweet, boneless little heap, Saana knew she was in all kinds of trouble.

It wasn't that the babies hadn't seemed real to her. They most definitely had—but in a completely intellectual and rather distant sense.

In her head, they had been Kenzie's babies. Nameless, faceless, future problems. They'd only become human—precious—in those fraught moments when Maria lifted them from the unconscious Kenzie's womb, and Saana had taken hold of them. Heard their first cries. Looked into their wrinkled, vernix-coated faces and seen not "the babies" but new and glorious lives filled with personality and potential.

Falling in love with them hadn't been high on Saana's list of priorities, but in those moments, she'd realized she hadn't been given a choice.

And she doubted she could love them any more than she already did.

After the nurses had chased her out of the room and were wheeling Kenzie to recovery, Saana had gone into the bathroom, locked the stall door, and cried from sheer and overwhelming emotion.

What had started as an act of altruism seemed set to be both the best and the worst thing she had ever done, but she was powerless to change any part of what had already gone.

And if she were honest, she didn't think she would, even if she could.

Mom cracked open the door cautiously, poking her head through just after Saana had put the babies back in their cot and, thankfully, redressed. Saana put her finger to her lips, pointing to where Kenzie lay asleep.

After a quick tiptoe closer to get a glimpse of Leanna and Darren, Mom gestured for Saana to come out into the corridor so they could talk.

"Have you decided on their names yet? When can I hold them? Are they letting McKenzie go home tomorrow or keeping her in longer?"

When Mom got this excited, it was sometimes hard to get a word in edgewise, so Saana held up both hands in surrender.

"Mom, slow down! Kenzie decided on Leanna and Darren, but there are no middle names yet. We discussed it and would like you to wait until at least tomorrow before you can cuddle them. And Dr. Ramcharam wants to keep Kenzie here at least three days to make sure there are no complications after the C-section."

"I'm so glad you got the bassinets when you did. I was telling your father that I have to get the nursery finished. It's mostly done. Just a few finishing touches. Things that hadn't been delivered yet but will be tomorrow. Oh, I can't wait to snuggle those babies."

Mom ran on for a while more, so enthusiastic neither of them had the heart to interrupt. Dad stood there, smiling the smile he reserved just for his live-wire wife, and Saana made all the appropriate noises while also keeping an eye on Kenzie through the glass at the top of the door.

"I'm not sure how long Kenzie will sleep," she said when Mom finally stopped to draw breath. "She's pretty exhausted."

"You look like you are too." Dad patted her shoulder. "When did you last eat?"

Saana shrugged, glancing back in at her sleeping wife. "Um, maybe around lunchtime?" She actually couldn't remember whether she had or not.

"If your mother promises not to actually touch the babies, why don't you let her sit with Mc-Kenzie for a while and you come with me to the cafeteria? You look like you need sustenance."

"I'm fine," she insisted. The memory of Kenzie's meltdown while trying to breastfeed was foremost in her mind. "But maybe I'll go get a cup of coffee. I'm planning to stay as long as they'll let me this evening."

"Go with your father." When Mom spoke in that tone of voice, it was a rare person who refused, no matter their age. "I'll just sit by the bed in case she wakes up, and I promise not to touch the babies. I'll just look."

Unable to find any good excuse not to do as ordered, Saana found herself walking down to the elevators with her father. Glancing across at his profile, Saana felt another jolt of tenderness, this time directed at the quiet, thoughtful man who had always been there for her, through thick or thin.

As her mother had often pointed out over the years, they were actually very much alike. Neither of them wore their heart on their sleeves but used logic to try to make sense of whatever life threw at them. Even when Saana didn't want to talk about things, she'd often found herself seeking out her father just to be around him. They'd play a game of golf or take the boat out and just spend the day hanging out.

And when she'd needed advice, he'd always been the one she turned to.

Riding down in the elevator, Saana leaned against the wall, fighting the feeling of being overwhelmed and scared by everything happening in her life. Trying, as she always did, to hide her fear. To be strong and reliable.

Kenzie and the babies needed her now more than they had before, and she knew she couldn't let them down.

"Parenthood is a scary job," Dad said after they'd sat at a table and Saana was nibbling on a rather unappetizing sandwich. "But just think of all the people who've done it, with varying levels of success, over the centuries, and it won't seem as frightening."

She tried to laugh, but it was a harsh, truncated sound that came from her throat, and her father's gaze sharpened.

"I know there's something going on you're not telling us about, Saana." He held up his hand when she opened her lips to speak, effectively stopping her. "You do know that whatever you need, your mother and I are there for you, don't you? And no matter how old you are, if there's anything you can't handle, we're here to lend a hand. The same goes for McKenzie."

Shaking her head, concentrating on the paper plate in front of her, she replied, "It's fine, Dad. Really. We just have a lot going on right now. Things we need to work out."

He tapped his fingers on his coffee cup and then took a sip before speaking.

"Both your mother and I have noticed how things have changed—how you have changed—since McKenzie came back. Not in a bad way—not at all—but in a good way. You're more relaxed, more well-balanced, less inclined to work yourself into the ground. But there's been a change in the…" He hesitated, as if looking for the right word. "A change in the dynamic between you two, and that is something I can't make up my mind about. It would be a good thing if it heralds maturity in both of you, but I can't be sure."

She forced a little laugh.

"We were in our thirties when we met, Dad. I'm a pretty well-respected doctor, and you heard what Kenzie has been through in her life. I don't think a lack of maturity is one of our problems."

He grimaced, leaving her to wonder if it was because of what she'd said or the taste of the coffee.

"You were sheltered, and somewhere along the line, you lost confidence in yourself as a person outside of your profession." He shrugged, and suddenly it was like looking into a mirror and seeing herself but in masculine form. "When you first introduced us to McKenzie, told us you were married, both your mother and I were understandably worried. You were obviously in love, and she was in love with you, but what the songwriters and poets don't tell you is that it's never enough. There has to be substance, understanding, the willingness to sacrifice and learn who the other person is, to back up the emotion.

"What we didn't see, back then, was a coming together—a meshing of lives, which always involves honesty and compromise. You were still working flat-out, as though nothing in your life had changed—"

"I was building my practice, Dad. Do you think I should have neglected it?"

"Neglected it? No. But there was no need to throw yourself into it so completely it was to the detriment of everything else in your life, including your marriage. Especially when you married a woman who must have needed your help to fit into a very different life than she was used to. She looked so uncomfortable all the time, Saana, and you didn't even seem to notice. When you told us she was going back to Texas to look after her aunt, I wondered if, in reality, she was running not so much away but back to a place that made sense to her."

Having lost her appetite, Saana pushed her plate away.

"You might be right, Dad, but things have changed. We have the babies now…"

Just saying it brought a rush of mingled love and fear and sorrow. She couldn't force anymore words past the burning lump in her throat.

"What's really going on?" Dad's voice had lost its softness and taken on a steel-sharp edge.

"I can't tell you." Now it was her time to don the cool, remote mask she used to shut out intrusion. "To do so would be to betray a trust and put us all—you included—in a bad spot. Don't ask me again, Dad."

For a long moment, their gazes clashed, battled, and then her father dipped his chin, apparently acknowledging her right to her secrets.

"All right, Saana. I won't push, but I will give you one piece of advice: decide what it is you want out of this relationship and then fight for it." Glancing at his watch, he tipped the last of his coffee into his mouth, then stood up. "We better get back up there before your mother can't help herself and starts petting those babies. I haven't seen her this excited since I don't know when. McKenzie's going to have to take a hard line with her, or she'll be moving in with you!"

From somewhere, Saana dredged up a smile and followed him back to the elevator, his words ringing in her head.

CHAPTER SEVENTEEN

HOME.

When on earth had she started thinking of the monstrous mansion in Indialantic that way, Kenzie wondered as the SUV drove through the gates, and she found herself sighing with relief.

Sore, still apprehensive about her new responsibilities, frankly overwhelmed, the last thing she expected was to view the house as a sanctuary, but that was exactly how she felt.

After driving around to the side of the house, Saana opened the garage door and drove inside.

"Just stay there a minute," she said as she turned off the engine. "And I'll come around to help you out before we liberate the babies."

Kenzie couldn't help chuckling at her turn of phrase.

"You make it sound like they're in jail rather than in their car seats."

Saana paused halfway out of the vehicle and said, "With what it took to get them into those seats, I think they are rather like prisons."

And Kenzie felt her heart lighten a little more.

Saana carried both the babies, still strapped into the detached seats, into the house, while Kenzie shuffled slowly along after her, feeling as if a truck had driven through her belly. By the time she got into the house, Saana had the elevator waiting so that Kenzie could step right into it.

"The first time I saw this thing, I thought it was ridiculous," she admitted. "Who on earth actually has an elevator in their house when there are only two floors? Now I've never been more grateful to the guy who put it in."

Saana snorted. "I have to agree with you. I don't think I've used it more than three or four times since I moved in, although when I was a child and visited my grandparents, Grandad used to lock it to stop me riding up and down in it all day."

She could almost picture it, and the mental image made Kenzie smile.

Everything seemed perfect at the moment. The babies being born healthy. Saana being attentive and helpful, far beyond what Kenzie would have expected. Not because she wasn't generous—nobody knew Saana's generous and giving nature better than she did—but she'd had the feeling during her pregnancy that Saana was keeping a mental distance. It was even in the way she'd always referred to them as "your babies," or "your children." Now, watching as she unstrapped and lifted Leanna out and placed the sleeping baby in the bassinet, there was no mistaking the tenderness in her every touch.

"Lie down," she said, nodding toward the bed. "Take a nap while these little ones sleep. You need your rest."

There it was again—that wonderful sense of being taken care of and treasured. A sensation she wasn't sure was real but was too incredibly tired to figure out.

And as the next few weeks passed, Kenzie found herself increasingly reluctant to do anything about either the Beauchamps or the situation between her and Saana. Instead, she took care of her children and basked in her in-laws' and, especially, Saana's gentle care. For the first time in her life, she felt part of a family complete rather than a lone wolf, circling the outskirts, hoping for scraps of connection.

Then she felt guilty for feeling that way. Hadn't Aunt Lena done the very best she could for her? Even when she had her own problems and issues and little time to cosset Kenzie in any way, she'd at least always been there.

She'd taken Saana's advice and hyphenated the surnames so the babies were registered as Bonham-Ameri, which actually sounded pretty good. If she and Saana were a real couple instead of in the midst of a crazy farce, Kenzie thought she'd change hers to that too.

But that wasn't in the cards. Not even to give her children a sense of belonging, knowing their mother shared the same name as them.

When Saana had brought it up again before the babies' names were registered, Kenzie had hesitated.

"What happens when we're no longer together? How do I explain it to them when they get older?"

That had gained her a shrug and a laconic reply.

"Kenzie, anything we do legally can be undone." After getting up, she'd walked across to look out the window and continued. "When the time comes, we can change the names back, if you want. Remember, right now we need to make it clear we're family."

It was then that the pleasant bubble of domesticity started to thin.

The lawyer had advised that rather than wait to be compelled to produce the birth certificates, they be proactive and send copies to the Beauchamps' attorney, which they did. Kenzie knew things would soon be coming to a head but refused to think about it too much. Enjoying this time with Saana, Leanna and Darren seemed far more important.

Saana was the one who consistently followed up with the lawyer, asking why they hadn't heard anything from their opponents.

"I thought we would have heard from them by now," she said. She had the lawyer on speaker, and was joggling Leanna on her shoulder while talking. "Either through their lawyer, or the courts. Do you have any idea what they might be doing?"

"None," the lawyer admitted. There was a bit of a hesitation, and then she added, "Perhaps they're trying to gather more information before they move."

Both Saana and Kenzie froze, exchanging a worried glance.

"Information? Like what?" Kenzie asked.

"I don't know for sure, but I don't think hiring a private investigator would be out of the question."

After that, Kenzie found herself scrutinizing every vehicle or person she noticed near the house.

"Do you think they might try to kidnap the children?" Saana asked Kenzie after they'd hung up, in that clear, cold way she had of speaking when she was really angry.

"I... I don't think so."

But her heart was pounding just from hearing the words.

"Don't worry," Saana said, putting her arm

around Kenzie's shoulders and pulling her in for a hug. "This is a secure neighborhood and house. Don't let it stress you out."

But after Saana went back to work, it was hard not to dwell on it, although Delores was there during the day to keep her company in between her chores.

"These babies are the sweetest," the housekeeper said almost daily, even though they were beginning to realize Miss Leanna already had a temper, which she wasn't afraid to unleash. If she was hungry or needed a diaper change, she didn't leave them in any doubt.

Darren was quieter, more easygoing.

"Takes after you," Saana said one night while they were lying on the bed together, both babies between them. "A laidback guy who doesn't want to cause any trouble."

Kenzie shook her head.

"You might want to rethink that statement," she said, only half joking. "You have to admit I've caused you—and keep on causing you—all kinds of trouble."

Saana only smiled, her brown eyes soft with an emotion Kenzie didn't know how to interpret. "Right now, lying here like this, I can honestly say I really don't mind."

Making Kenzie remember exactly why she'd fallen so hard for Saana and how much it was going to hurt to give her up again.

* * *

Impatient didn't begin to describe the way Saana felt as she hung up the phone after talking with the lawyer yet again.

She'd set herself a weekly reminder to call the woman in San Antonio, and never failed to make contact for a status update.

No doubt the recipient of her Friday-morning calls was probably getting fed up, but if they didn't get the question of Leanna and Darren's custody settled soon, she thought she might lose it.

There'd been time during her leave to think long and hard about what her father had said the night the babies were born. To look back at those early days and—with the new insight she'd gained into Kenzie's character and her own—figure out some of where things went wrong.

He'd been right to say she hadn't done much to help Kenzie assimilate into her new life. If she were honest, with unconcern and arrogance, it hadn't even occurred to her that either her wealth or her ambition would be a problem. While she'd been ecstatic to realize Kenzie had no interest in her money, deep inside, there'd been part of her that secretly thought her wife was actually happy to have married into wealth.

After all, wasn't that pretty much standard? And everyone knew having too much money was far better than having too little.

But that wasn't Kenzie. What Saana had put down as an almost ridiculous level of independence was actually a self-defense mechanism. One that had allowed her to somehow survive and thrive in a situation that would break most other children.

Kenzie may have loved and been grateful to her aunt, but in Saana's book, the older woman had done the minimum while expecting the maximum in return. Not that she'd ever say that to Kenzie. No. Now that Lena was gone, it was best to let it all lie.

Instead, it was time to look to the future. And that wouldn't be possible the way Saana wanted until the custody battle was over. To her way of thinking, that needed to be settled before she could ask Kenzie to stay and keep this beautiful family they'd somehow ended up creating intact.

In the meantime, she was doing her best to show Kenzie how much she cared about her and their children. Because she really did think of them as hers as well as Kenzie's. Every day, each time she looked at them, cuddled or played with them, she fell in love a little more. When she looked back at the night they were born, when she arrogantly assumed her feelings for them were already at their peak, she had to laugh at herself.

She honestly couldn't imagine her life without

them. Without Kenzie. She'd do any and everything in her power to protect them all.

Why, why, why hadn't the Beauchamps already made their move?

Until they did, they were all stuck in limbo instead of being able to move forward.

Even though she was back at work, she'd rearranged her schedule to avoid the twelve-hour days she'd been working and found, to her relief and chagrin, that both clinics continued to function perfectly well.

Apparently, she wasn't as completely irreplaceable as she'd so conceitedly thought. Tonight she was working at the Eau Galle clinic, and one of her patients was Miriam Durham, who'd been Kenzie's first patient at the clinic. They'd been able to diagnose her with hypothyroidism and had put her on a course of treatment that seemed to be working well.

By now, not only did everyone working at the clinic know Kenzie was Saana's wife but somehow, through the grapevine, many of the patients did too. Including Miriam.

So it was no surprise when the first thing she asked when Saana entered the examination room was, "How's your wife? Got any pictures?"

Laughing, Saana pulled out her phone, asking, "Do seagulls steal your lunch? Here're the latest. I took them last night."

And Miriam *ooh*ed and *ahh*ed over them until

Saana insisted they talk about her disease and treatment schedule rather than the babies.

"I got your latest blood-test results back, and I think the dosage of the medicine is working well," she said after she'd taken a look at her vitals. "Are you seeing any improvement in the joint pain and fatigue?"

"Oh, yes." Miriam beamed. "I feel so much better already. Hard to recognize myself after only two months on the meds. I'm even able to work a full shift and then go to the park or visit with friends. Before, all I could do was go home and collapse on the couch."

Saana took another look at Kenzie's notes from the first visit Miriam had made to the clinic, seeing *Depression over alienation from son/grandchildren.*

"And how're things with your son? Are you seeing him and his children more often?"

Miriam's smile wavered slightly, but Saana, although watching carefully, didn't see any signs of sadness.

"Still on and off, but things are gettin' a bit better, I think. It's hard on us all because it would be easier on Marlon and his wife if I could take care of the kids regularly, but I can't just yet. I told him about what you said and how much I've improved so far, and I think he'll talk to his wife about me seein' my babies when I'm not working."

Talking to Miriam once more brought home to Saana just what the Beauchamps must be feeling, but she had to put that aside so as not to get distracted.

"I hope it works out for you and your grandbabies," she said, gaining herself another broad smile.

The clinic ran late, so it was almost ten o'clock before Saana headed home. She yawned, glad she wasn't working the next day. She'd made the decision to keep the weekends free as much as possible, although loosening the reins of her businesses had created some anxiety. However, she told herself hopefully, it was just as well she start doing that now so that when the kids got older and had weekend activities, she could be involved.

She was almost home when her phone rang, and her heart leapt when she saw her father's number. Pressing the button on the steering wheel to answer, she slowed down, pulling close to the curb.

"Dad? Is everything okay? Is Mom okay?"

"We're both fine," he said, but there was more than a hint of steel in his voice. "But I need to speak to you—and McKenzie."

"Now? I'm pretty sure Kenzie is sleeping already. Leanna and Darren wake up at all hours, so she'd taken to turning in early."

She was babbling, worried by that tone in his

voice and the fact he wanted to speak to them both rather than just her.

"It can wait until tomorrow morning, but I wanted to make sure you'll be at home when I get there. It's important."

"Why not just tell me what it's about instead of all this cloak-and-dagger business?"

He was silent for a long minute, and then Saana thought she heard him exhale.

"I just got off the phone with a man named Andrew Beauchamp. He told me a story about his son and McKenzie, and seems completely convinced that your marriage is a sham."

Saana stopped the car, too intent on the conversation to pay attention to where she was going.

"Really." Her brain was whirling, and cold rage made her fingers tighten in a vise grip on the steering wheel. "Did he say where he got that erroneous information?"

"He didn't say, and I didn't press him. That part of it seemed irrelevant to me."

"So what did he say he wanted?"

"He asked me to help him get custody of his grandchildren. I refused, of course, but what I need to know is why the *hell* you didn't tell me what was going on from before?"

CHAPTER EIGHTEEN

KENZIE WOKE UP at the first mewling coming from the bassinet and rubbed her eyes before sitting up. The room was still dark, with just a hint of dawn at the edge of the curtain and the glow of the nightlight.

"I'm coming, Mr. D.," she whispered, glad to be woken up by his soft sounds rather than her daughter's lusty howls.

Glancing over, she realized Saana's side of the bed was empty and wondered where she was. Usually, on the mornings she didn't have to work, she would lie in bed with them while Kenzie nursed the babies, either singly or in tandem.

Because Darren woke up first and wasn't fussy, Kenzie was able to change his diaper before his sister set to howling. After a quick diaper change for Leanna, too, Kenzie made herself comfortable and fed them both.

There was still no sign of Saana, so when the babies fell back to sleep, Kenzie put on a robe and went downstairs to look for her.

She eventually looked out toward the river and saw her sitting on one of the benches, bent forward with her elbows on her knees. Something about her posture made Kenzie's stomach drop, and for a moment, she considered going back upstairs.

Pretending she hadn't noticed her out there.

Then, telling herself she was being silly, she let herself out of the house and walked down the path, her flip-flops almost silent on the gravel.

It felt like a full-circle moment but in reverse. Rather than her sitting on the bench, wondering what to do next, it was Saana.

But there wasn't anything for Saana to decide, was there?

As she got closer, her wife straightened and glanced back for an instant.

"Hey. You're up early."

"Yes. I couldn't sleep and didn't want to disturb you, so I went downstairs." Ordinary words, but her tone was off. Cool, but in a newer, icier form. Kenzie shivered. "The babies woke you up?"

"Yes." Strangely weak-kneed, she sat on the other bench. "I fed them, and they've gone back to sleep. What's wrong?"

Saana rubbed her knuckles under her nose, a gesture so unlike her usual poise that fingers of cold ran down Kenzie's spine.

"I've finally found out what the Beauchamps' next move will be. Actually, *has* been."

Kenzie's mouth went dry, and she felt light-headed but forced herself to inhale deeply—once, twice, three times. When she knew she wouldn't pass out, she licked her lips and asked, "What happened?"

"Mr. Beauchamp called Dad last night. Told him that our marriage wasn't real and asked for his help 'convincing' you to give up the babies."

Maybe she should be panicking, she wasn't sure. But instead, a deep, numbing calm came over her.

"Oh."

Saana looked over at her, and when their gazes clashed, Kenzie couldn't read her wife's expression. It reminded her of the night of the gala, when Saana had listened to the story of Kenzie's young life and said nothing, hiding her reaction.

"Dad wants to talk to us, so he's coming over this morning." Her lips tightened, and her nostrils flared on a breath. "What do you want to tell him? We need to get our stories straight."

This was it, then. The moment she'd known instinctively would one day come, no matter how she'd dreamed it wouldn't or pretended to herself that it would never come about.

"We tell him the truth. Your father—your parents—deserve that."

No matter how much they might hate her for it.

Saana nodded, turning to look back over the water again, as yet untouched by the weak dawn light, so dark and gloomy looking, fitting the mood of their conversation perfectly.

She wanted to ask if she should pack and leave; if Saana would expect that of her, but the words stuck in her throat. Funny how initially she'd been completely prepared to raise the babies by herself, but now the prospect filled her with pain.

No one needed to tell her how much Saana loved Leanna and Darren. It was obvious in every interaction, in the gentleness that went beyond just an adult being careful with a child. The tender way she looked at them, spoke to them, held them.

Losing them would devastate her, but what was the alternative? Because they were a package deal—the babies and her—and Saana couldn't have one without the other.

No matter how much she loved her wife, Kenzie wasn't willing to give her children up to her just to make her happy, and Saana had given no indication she wanted Kenzie to stay. Not to stay for the sake of the babies, but because Saana wanted her for herself.

A while ago, she'd suggested Kenzie consider staying in Florida, letting the Ameris stay in contact and continue to act as grandparents. But that seemed even less viable than it had in the past.

Back then, they'd viewed Kenzie as their daughter-in-law. A part of the family. Now that they knew it had all been a lie, why would they want anything to do with her or her kids?

Suddenly, Kenzie realized she was shivering, almost hard enough to make her teeth chatter, and she got up, pulling the neck of her robe closer to her throat.

"I'm goin' inside. What time is your father comin' over?"

Saana shrugged. "He didn't say, but I suspect it'll be quite early. I know he wants to sort this out ASAP."

"Okay."

That was the best she could manage. The adult part of her was saying she should stay. That they needed to talk this out. But the little girl wanted to run and hide, the way she had in the past when things got too hard to handle.

She needed time to think, is what she told herself. But even as she walked back to the house, she knew the truth.

This was nothing more or less than the ultimate coward's escape.

Saana couldn't remember a time when she'd been quite so angry. Enraged, really.

It wasn't just a matter of her and Kenzie having their hand forced, but even more so the violation implicit in Mr. Beauchamp's actions. He'd clearly had them watched. Investigated. How else would he have known to contact her parents?

Was that even legal, since both sides had lawyers involved? Even if it was, it was underhanded in the extreme. The type of maneuver men of wealth and power probably wouldn't hesitate to use when up against women, in the hopes of intimidating them into compliance.

But while Saana's brain was going too fast just then for the kind of cool planning needed, there was one thing she knew for sure.

The Beauchamps had bitten off more than they could chew.

Where previously she'd had some sympathy for them, now she was ready to plot their downfall.

Family was everything, and by messing with hers—spying, and scaring, and overstepping the bounds of decency—they'd set themselves up for a bitter disappointment.

Family.

In the past, that had been her parents, grandparents and brother. Now… Now her whole heart and soul was up there in the house, and she wasn't going to give any of it up without a fight.

She loved Kenzie. Always had. But now she had a deeper understanding of what made her tick, what her fears might be, what they needed to make a go of their life together. It meant not only stepping outside of her sexual inhibitions, the way Kenzie had taught her, but also outside of her emotional ones too.

Opening up, expressing her feelings, no matter how raw or ugly, wasn't something Saana was good at. She'd rather hide behind cool logic, even when she was a screaming mass of emotion inside.

But she couldn't help remembering what her father had said the night the babies were born. The things he said every relationship needed to survive and thrive.

Honesty.

Communication.

Compromise.

Willingness to sacrifice.

He'd intimated that for all she'd achieved, she'd never fully grown up. But now she knew that if there was ever a time to do so, with her marriage and her family—her children—on the line, this was it.

And she'd have to start with Kenzie.

Enigmatic Kenzie, who also had the uncanny knack of keeping her own council, leaving Saana guessing as to how she really felt when things got serious. How arrogant Saana had been when she so blithely assumed that Kenzie's easygoing ways made her simple to read. She was anything but simple or easy. In fact, she was one of the most complex women Saana had ever met.

Sitting up suddenly, she wondered what that

complicated mind was thinking and planning right now. Was Kenzie's mind spinning the way Saana's was, trying to come up with an answer to the problems they'd created?

Did that answer include keeping their family together or tearing it apart?

That thought had her on her feet in an instant and almost running toward the house.

She took the stairs two at a time, tearing into the bedroom, coming to a halt when she found it empty except for the babies, still asleep in their cots. And checking the walk-in closet proved unfruitful, so she went across to open the door to the nursery.

Kenzie was standing just inside the room, her arms crossed tightly over her waist, looking at the mural Mom had commissioned. It depicted a southwestern landscape, made dreamy by the light colors used, with a variety of animals scattered throughout. While it certainly wasn't a traditional baby's room look because of the palette and subject matter, it really worked.

"I love it," Kenzie said, and Saana couldn't miss the sadness in her voice. "Your mom really outdid herself, didn't she?"

"Yes." Saana edged closer until she was directly behind Kenzie. "I'm glad you love it. And it'll be good for word illustration too. Leanna and Darren's first words will probably be *horse* instead of *mama*."

The shuddering breath Kenzie took was audible. "I'm not leaving them here with you. I'll keep fighting for them, and when I go, they'll be coming with me."

Shocked, Saana said, "What are you talking about?"

Kenzie spun around to face her, and the sorrow on her face was unmistakable.

"I know you love the babies, and your parents do too. And I also know y'all probably despise me for all the chaos I've caused and want me to leave. I'll go, Saana, but I can't leave my babies behind, even though I know you can give them a far better life than I could."

Shaking her head, Saana said, "Nobody is going to tell you to give up your babies, Kenzie, me least of all. I'm ready to fight with everything I have to make sure Leanna and Darren grow up with their mama—with you."

Kenzie's lips parted, but before she could speak, Saana put a finger against her lips, halting the words.

"I need to tell you something else. I love you. I've always loved you. And I know I haven't always been what you've needed, but if you love me and decide to stay with me, I'll do whatever I can to make it up to you. You don't have to say anything now, just bear all that in mind when you're deciding what you want to do."

Kenzie shook her head, not saying anything, just as the doorbell rang.

"That must be Dad. I'll go let him in. Will you come down?"

Kenzie's chin lifted even though her eyes were damp, and her voice was shaky when she replied, "Of course. I just need to change. But, Saana…"

Her voice faded, and Saana held up her hand as she went through the door, saying, "Later. We'll talk later."

There was no way she'd be able to hold it together if Kenzie rejected her right now, and she wanted to present a strong front for her father.

To her surprise, when she got downstairs, she found both her parents on the doorstep. Dad looked furious, while Mom looked like she'd been crying.

"Come in," she said, and then, when they were both inside, she kissed them each on the cheek. "Let's go into the kitchen. Kenzie's just changing, and the babies are sleeping. Do you want some coffee?" she asked as they walked down the hallway.

With habitual politeness, both her parents refused, and Mom started a rambling dialogue of small talk as they each took a seat around the kitchen table.

Surreal, to be acting as if there was nothing wrong, when nothing felt right and wouldn't feel right until she knew what Kenzie wanted to do.

They'd just sat down, Mom still rambling on, when Kenzie came down the back staircase, pausing just at the bottom for an instant. Mom spluttered to silence as Kenzie walked over to sit.

Holding up her hand, she said, "I have somethin' I want to say, before we get into the nitty-gritty of this crazy situation." Suddenly, Saana found herself the focus of her wife's gaze, and her heart began to race. "I love you, Saana. I loved you from the first moment I looked up and saw you standin' in front of me on the bus to Hoover Dam, and I'm pretty damn sure I'll love you forever.

"I didn't realize it, when I lit out from Texas, comin' back here to you, but I was runnin' towards the one person who made me feel safe. The one person I knew I could trust and depend on. I didn't know whether you'd want me back or not, but I knew you'd help me if you could."

Suddenly, Saana didn't even care that her parents were sitting there, watching. She needed to kiss her wife, so buoyed by relief she felt her happiness would cause her to float off into heaven.

When she leaned forward, Kenzie met her halfway, and they exchanged a long kiss, redolent of love, spiced with their passion and sweetened by newly renewed commitment.

As their lips parted, Dad cleared his throat and said, "Well, I'm glad that's all dealt with. Now, what are we going to do about the Beauchamps?"

CHAPTER NINETEEN

KENZIE KNEW MR. AMERI was a businessman, but it had never really sunk in just how serious he could be. Each time they'd met before, he'd been in gracious host or laidback-father mode. Now, suddenly, with what he seemed to perceive as a threat to his family, his nice-guy persona fell away to be replaced by a pit bull.

She couldn't believe she'd ever hear herself defend the Beauchamps in any way, but when Mr. Ameri started talking about suing them for slander, she felt she had to intervene.

"It's not that I don't understand how they feel," she explained. "Darryl was their only son, and I know losing him was a horrible blow, but they just assumed I'd hand the babies over without any conversation. As if they were entitled to them."

"Bullies is what they are. I can't stand a bully. They should have given some thought to what they would do if someone started messing around and threatening *their* family before they decided to mess with ours. Don't worry, McKenzie, I'll take care of it."

Hearing him say it that way had made her quite emotional. The Ameri family was claiming her as one of their own, circling the wagons around her and the babies, and the feeling was wonderful.

"Don't worry," Saana murmured so her parents couldn't hear. "Mom will be the voice of reason. Once Dad calms down, she'll work on him and make sure he doesn't go off the rails."

"Go off the rails?"

Saana chuckled. "When he fixates on something, especially if he believes he's righting a wrong, he sometimes doesn't know when to stop. Mom will redirect him to the appropriate solution."

Somehow, knowing the Ameris were behind her somewhat lessened the fear she'd harbored that the Beauchamps would find a way to take her children. It was becoming obvious neither Saana nor her father would ever allow that to happen, and so she felt she could consider a compromise.

"I don't mind letting them see the babies— have some kind of relationship—but the visits would have to be supervised when they're little."

"Definitely not." Mr. Ameri's voice was cool and controlled even though Kenzie knew he was anything but inside.

Now she knew where Saana got that particular characteristic.

Mrs. Ameri just shook her head and said nothing until Leanna let out a lusty yowl from upstairs, and she asked if she could go up with Kenzie.

"I was hoping they would wake up before we had to go," she said when Kenzie happily agreed. "I do love them so."

"I'm glad you do," Kenzie admitted. "Everyone needs family."

Mrs. Ameri picked Leanna up and checked her diaper.

"Oh, darling. You're absolutely soaked. Let's get you cleaned up. Is it feeding time yet?"

"I shouldn't think so," Kenzie replied, following Mrs. Ameri over to the changing table. "We'll know once she's dry. If she stops crying, then you know she isn't hungry."

Sure enough, once she was changed, she lay quietly in Grandma's arms, kicking her legs for a few minutes before nodding off. Mrs. Ameri settled in the upholstered chair and happily rocked the sleeping baby.

It felt like the right time to speak to her while they were alone, in case she wanted to say anything she didn't wish Saana to hear.

"Mrs. Ameri, I want to thank you for accepting me into the family the way you have. I know I'm not in the same league as Saana—"

The older lady clicked her tongue. "We love you, Kenzie, and think you're good for Saana. If you make her happy, that's all I'm interested in."

And one more small corner of her battered heart was healed.

Later that evening, after Saana's parents had gone home and the babies had been bathed and fed, they lay side by side on the bed, Kenzie holding Darren, and Saana, Leanna. The atmosphere in the room radiated peace, and the love both of them had tried to deny and now finally acknowledged and reveled in.

"What a day," she said. "Stressful and amazing, all at the same time."

Saana gave her a long look.

"I want to say something, and I want you to believe me."

Kenzie's heart did a little flip, but she held Saana's gaze as she nodded.

"Mom had a word with me before she left, telling me that I'd obviously omitted to explain exactly how I feel about you, since you're still worried about what she delicately termed our 'difference in backgrounds.'"

"Oh, Lawdie. I love your mom, but I wish she hadn't said anything."

Saana shook her head, and she didn't smile. Instead, her gaze was intense and serious.

"I've never cared about where you came from, how you dress or any of that. The first time I saw you, all I noticed was how beautiful you were. When we started speaking, I felt I'd found something I hadn't even known I needed—a friend, love, a home for my soul. It never even occurred to me that our backgrounds would have any bearing at all on our relationship. If I had, I'd have told you about the money and all of it. But just like you never thought it was important to tell me about your parents and what you'd experienced as a child, I didn't think my wealth would make a difference."

Then she took a deep breath and straightened slightly before she continued.

"Actually, if I'm honest, I arrogantly thought if my wealth was going to make a difference, it would be in a good way rather than a bad. I apologize for that, and also for not giving you the attention and help you needed to actually settle in when you moved here."

Kenzie exhaled, her heart steadying from the rolling gallop it had taken up when Saana started to speak. It took a moment to work through all Saana had said and figure out what she, in turn, needed to say. All the time, Saana was watching her, and Kenzie felt her gaze like the warmth of the sun.

"I think, looking back, that it was a good thing you didn't tell me how rich you were when we met," she admitted. "If you had, I probably wouldn't have gotten involved with you. Everything about this house, the way you lived, made me feel small and worthless, but I know that was my lack of confidence rather than anything you did."

It was a hard thing to admit, but she felt strong enough—safe enough—to unburden all the emotions she'd been hiding.

"When I left to go take care of Aunt Lena, I really meant to come back. But when I got to Texas, I fell back into my old way of life, and the longer I stayed, the harder it became to imagine ever belongin' here. Every conversation with you felt like it was happening over a wider distance every time. Eventually, I just couldn't do it anymore. It just hurt too bad.

"I know I hurt you by staying away and not taking your calls or staying in contact, but I honestly believed you were better off without me."

"Oh, babe." The pain in Saana's voice was evident, and when she brushed the back of her hand across Kenzie's cheek, it felt like a benediction. "I'll do whatever it takes to make you comfortable. We can sell the house, if you want. Move into somewhere more to your taste."

Now, without a doubt, Kenzie knew Saana truly loved her if she was willing to give up her beloved family home. But it didn't seem important anymore.

"No." She gave her wife a soft smile, so filled

with love her throat was tight. "I'm happy here, with you, now. And I know how much you love it."

Saana shook her head slowly, her lips twitching, as though she wasn't sure whether to laugh or do something else.

"You never did say whether you'd stay with me or not." Now the movement of her lips was clearly caused by suppressed laughter. "If you don't want to live with me, you could always move in with my parents. I think they love you more than me."

"Nah. Love 'em, but they don't make my heart pound or make me think naughty thoughts."

Saana laughed lightly then. "Glad to hear it. That's my job."

"I'm sorry, babe, but you're truly stuck with me." Leaning close, she gave Saana a lingering kiss, and when it ended, she whispered, "I'm here to stay."

EPILOGUE

KENZIE LOOKED AROUND the room, trying to find her boots.

"Don't tell me I left them at home," she muttered to herself as she rummaged through the cupboard where her clothes had been stowed. Then, with an exclamation of satisfaction, she found them. "Thank goodness!"

Outside the window, there was a steady stream of chatter from the Ameris' garden, and from down the hall came a sudden shriek she recognized as what they called *Leanna denied*. Quickly pulling on the white cowboy boots, she went out into the hall.

There, she saw Delores trying to wrangle a squirming Leanna, who was firmly embedded in the terrible twos. When combined with that temper she'd been exhibiting since birth, it had become a particularly trying time.

"Leanna Mariella," she called. "Please behave yourself."

"Mama!" Darren was the one who came running toward her, arms outstretched, to be picked up. "Ms. Delores said there was cake, but Lee-Lee and me haven't got any."

"Ahh." Now she understood the problem. "Nobody's had cake yet, and nobody will until after dinner."

Coming toward her, Leanna in tow, Delores gave Kenzie a grin.

"I shouldn't have mentioned it, but it seemed like a good idea at the time."

Kenzie shook her head, returning the older woman's smile as she placed Darren back onto his feet. "You shoulda known better."

"I should," came the reply as Delores took Darren's hand. "Come on, let's go downstairs you two. Your moms will be coming down soon." She raised an eyebrow in Kenzie's direction. "Right?"

Kenzie chuckled. "I'll go and hurry Saana along, or who knows how long the guests will have to wait."

True to form, when Kenzie entered Saana's room, it was to find her wife almost dressed but struggling with her zipper.

"Babe, everyone is waiting for us to come down. Why aren't you ready?"

"I'm almost ready," Saana said, smiling and looking totally unrepentant. "Oh, you look delicious."

Kenzie smoothed her hand down the silk of

her cream jacket, enjoying the slip of the fabric against her palm. The lovely sensation reminded her of Saana's skin.

"You look real tasty yourself."

They'd decided to wear outfits made from the same cream fabric, but although Kenzie had opted for a pantsuit, Saana looked elegant in a sheath dress. Both were trimmed with a hint of gold thread, adding to the festive nature of the outfits.

Perfect for a blessing ceremony and renewal of their vows.

"Lift your arm, and let me zip you in," Kenzie said, stepping close to fit deed to words. "Did you remember your earrings?"

"Yes. I just have to find them."

As she hunted for them, Kenzie went to the window and looked out at where their guests were waiting.

Mrs. Ameri was shooing everyone toward the chairs, which were set out in a semicircular pattern. Even from this distance, Kenzie could pick out most of the people there. They'd opted for a small ceremony rather than a large bash. After all, this was their fifth anniversary, and neither of them wanted anyone there who wasn't terribly important to them personally.

"You better hurry. Your mom is getting everyone settled, and you know how punctual she is."

"Are the Beauchamps here?"

"Yeah. I see them down there."

It had taken some time, but they'd come to terms with the Beauchamps, and the older couple had agreed to come to Florida to see their grandchildren periodically. Maybe, when Leanna and Darren were older, they'd be allowed to go visit in Texas, but it wouldn't be for a while. While everything seemed on the up-and-up, both Kenzie and Saana had trust issues about them.

It was hard to forget what they'd been willing to do to take the children.

"Happy, love?"

Saana came up behind her, fitting her body against Kenzie's back, her arms around her waist.

"Ecstatic," Kenzie admitted, smiling with the realization it was true. "I'm about to marry the woman I love all over again. I can't think of anything better."

Saana's arms tightened fractionally.

"Neither can I. Shall we go?"

"Yes. Let's. I can't wait to kiss the bride."

She turned and faced Saana's sweet, seductive smile.

"You don't have to wait, you know."

And Saana had to reapply her lipstick before they could go down to join their family and friends and once more pledge their love to each other.

* * * * *